"One Hand Washes The Other"

A Novella

By

Bernard Snyder

"About The Author"

After experiencing great success with my previous five Non-Fiction books and having my best-seller, "Ahead of My Time" being distributed in five different countries around the world (Thanks in large part to the late Scott Horn, the generous maintenance man at McDonald's on Hilton Head, who generously bought each intern a copy of my book for them to take back to their respective countries), I decided to do something different. I decided to write a Novella. For those of you that didn't' know, I was born in Savannah, Georgia, and raised on beautiful, Hilton Head Island, S.C. I have three lovely daughters who are all college graduates. Thanks in large part to their mother, Anginette, who has been nothing short of amazing in my daughters becoming the bright, intelligent, and successful women they've become. At a very young age, I dreamt of becoming an author. It wasn't until I was laughed at by a child-hood friend with whom I'd shared that dream I found the motivation to make the dream a reality. That very friend with whom I'd not only shared my dream, but most of my teen years playing basketball with, unknowingly became my biggest motivator. The inspiration for which this book was written came from an unlikely source. It was a breezy Saturday night on Hilton Head. I decided to take a joy ride to the local convenience store. This is where I stumbled into a gentleman on the corner. The man introduced himself and told me he felt as if he knew me well. He said, "I just finished reading your autobiography, "The Perfect Triangle." I asked him if he liked what he'd read? The gentleman answered, "I'm not sure if anyone has ever told you what I'm about to say, Mr. Snyder, but if you ever decide to write a movie or screenplay, no telling how far you could go." Those words, along with a few inspiring people I've met along my journey, became the contributing factors for which "One Hand Washes the Other' was created.

By
Bernard Snyder

Dedication

I dedicate this book to my dear first cousin, Edward 'Byrd' Snider who passed away just a few months ago. You will be dearly missed... may your soul rest in peace.

INTRODUCTION:

"One Hand Washes the Other"

This is the story of two friends, Edward Keats and Marcus Irvin Anderson. They grew up together in Decatur, Georgia. Both were raised by their mothers after the untimely death of their fathers, who lost their lives in separate car accidents on busy I-285 a year apart. Edward and Marcus were alike in many ways. They were both incredibly talented and determined, had similar aspirations, and some would even say they were more like brothers than friends. At an early age, Marcus taught himself how to play a guitar. He became so good at it that it would become his primary source of income at one point. Edward was considered the smarter of the two and according to his peers, the one most likely to succeed. Edward was also known as the modern-day Shakespeare because of his God-gifted ability at Poetry. Though he'd never had any of his work published, everyone who knew him assumed his work would eventually be seen in art galleries around the world. As kids, both decided they didn't like their mothers having to catch the city bus to and from work in horrible weather conditions. They were too young to make a difference at the time, but they knew when they got old enough to change things, they would. Meanwhile, they needed to work on a plan. They made an agreement amongst themselves that whatever plan they'd come up with, they would have each other's back no matter what. A fatal tragedy occurs. The culprits behind this tragedy are mysterious. With no known suspects or clear motive as to who committed the crime, the case seems unsolvable. Surprisingly, it was the intuition of a street-smart friend that would lead to a shocking discovery and an ending that would leave you on the edge of your seat!

By
Bernard Snyder

Table of Contents

"Special Thanks"

As always, I'd like to give thanks to God first and foremost. Without him, none of this would be possible. My books have reached parts of the world I've never dreamed of. They've inspired folks I've never actually met in person. One particular fan pulled me to the side a few years ago. She said, "Bernard, I have a confession to make. I haven't had a chance to read your entire book (*"Ahead of My Time"*) but only because I rewrote one of your poems and gave it to my husband, who hasn't been himself lately. As I handed the poem to him, I said, "This is how I still feel about you." My husband read the poem and teared up, and ever since that day, we've been traveling and having fun again. I would like to take this time to thank you. I do believe your words saved my marriage, Bernard." That conversation alone told me I made a difference in at least two people's lives. My writing has connected me with amazing people all over the world. I know in my heart I couldn't have done any of this alone. I am forever grateful to the Almighty. He has allowed me to live my dream as an author, which I am proud of. He has also provided me the determination to write five Non-fiction books, one of which is an autobiography, *"The Perfect triangle"*, which is in discussion of becoming a movie. God inspires me to do what I do. I don't take his presence for granted, not even for a second. Often times I've been asked, "How are you able to do what you do without parental guidance or a college education?" I simply smile and say, "I am never alone. Even though you can't see my mentor, he is always present. He has been by my side throughout my entire journey. And for that, I am never alone, I am at peace, and I am forever thankful."

CHAPTER ONE
Natalie Owens

I grew up in Morgantown, West Virginia. I attended Marshall University, graduated as the top student in my class, and earned my bachelor's Degree. As a graduation gift, my dad, Fred Owens ("FO" is what everyone in the neighborhood calls him) bought me a brand-new Toyota Camry. I am an only child, so everyone seems to think I've been a spoiled brat all of my life. Which is far from the truth. My parents, Wilma and Fred Owens have always supported me in whatever goal I tried to attain. I absolutely love my parents dearly. I feel if they weren't as supportive as they've been, I wouldn't be as far along in life as I am. We are very much alike, yet, so very different. My parents seem to have this strong dislike for people of color. I never understood where this came from until one day while my parents were watching the Evening News, I told them I had a very serious question to ask that I would need an honest answer to. My mother muted the television so I could have their full attention. I told them I needed to know where this prejudice against people of color originated from. My mother seemed shocked that I would ask such a question. My dad, on the other hand, became furious, as if the question jolted a cold secret from his memory bank from years back. He said, "People of color, particularly Blacks, aren't any good. They're only good at two things in this world. Those two things happen to be playing Sports and having Sex." At this point, I watched as my mother covered her face with both hands as if this was a topic previously discussed between the two of them.

Natalie

My dad continued, "Blacks are inferior to us. As a matter of fact, I don't even like Black Coffee, and to be quite honest, I've never had a Black friend, and I prefer you not have any of them as friends either." I immediately yelled back at my dad, "You cannot tell me who I should or shouldn't have as friends. You don't have that right." My dad quickly responded, "You don't have the right to talk sassy to me in my own house." This argument went back and forth for all of ten minutes. Suddenly, you could hear a pin drop. At this point, my mother slowly removed her hands from her face. I could tell she'd been crying. It was as if I could see the guilt in my mother's eyes after the tears had dried up. My mother grabbed my hand and asked if she could have a word with me in my bedroom. "Sure, why not," I said. I could sense this conversation would be one my mother and I had never discussed before. I entered my bedroom. My mother closely followed. She closed the door behind her as if she didn't want our conversation to seep in my dad's direction. We sat on the edge of my bed. "I would like you to listen to my entire story without any interruptions, understood?" mom whispered. "No problem," I said.

Natalie

My mother continued whispering, "Natalie, my dear, I am the one to blame for your father thinking the way he does. You see, before I met your father, I dated a Black man. His name was Nathaniel, but I affectionately called him Natbo. Natbo and I fell in love. Our relationship was odd, to say the least. Our main problem was society never accepted us as a couple. Back then, and even in some places here now, a white person dating anyone outside of his or her race is frowned upon. The people here in West Virginia are set in their ways. Well, Natbo didn't want anything bad to happen to me. So, one night, we met up at one of our secret spots. We discussed the dangers we have to deal with on a daily basis, society's perception of us, and the disappointing fact that we could never be happy as a couple here in West Virginia. We both agreed it would be best if he left the city altogether. Natbo didn't have enough money to take me with him to another state, so I asked him to go on without me, and if we are meant to be together, we will. I also asked him to hold me and make love to me for what might be our very last time. He complied with my wishes, and afterward, he kissed me goodbye. As hard as it was to let him go, I knew it was the right decision. Years later, I met your dad, "FO." A few months into our relationship, 'FO' and I were out drinking, and in the midst of, perhaps, five or six 'Vodka Tonics, we decided to have a heart-to-heart conversation about years gone by, and I foolishly shared my story with him. Even though it was some years ago, the thought of me and Natbo's relationship never set well with your dad. I haven't seen nor heard from Natbo since that night he left, but your dad has always had a hard time dealing with that particular story of my past. Fast forwarding, your dad asked me about Natbo again six months later. I knew how insecure he was about Natbo, so I assured him there was no need to concern himself with Natbo or any other man. I clearly stated that I haven't seen Natbo, nor do I plan to. My comment did seemed to have eased your dad's concerns momentarily. Yet, of all the things I discussed pertaining to my past, your dad chose to only remember that Natbo walked away as if I was left in the dark. The truth of the matter is, your dad didn't like that I had nothing bad to say about Natbo. And on that particular night, your dad and I went out drinking, I didn't have a problem telling your dad how I still felt about Natbo. Of course, your dad did listen to my entire story, but he would only choose the portions of my story he wanted to remember. Which seemed to allow him to think whatever he wanted, and I didn't want to waste my time or energy trying to change his mindset.

Natalie

My mom's story had me in tears. I didn't know what to think. I just sat there in a daze. My mother grabbed my hand and added these words," Natalie, I want you to move away and see the world. I would hate to see you stuck here in West Virginia, where society's perception could cloud your future as it did mine. See, 'Natbo' made me feel 'something' I'd never felt with anyone else. I can say with confidence I don't think I would ever experience that type of feeling ever again. But, as for you, you're young, attractive, intelligent, and your entire life lies ahead of you. I would like for you to pursue your dreams, whatever they are, live life to the fullest, and date or marry whomever you choose. There's a bigger world out there, but living here in West Virginia, you wouldn't know it because everything here is viewed on how things have always been rather than how things have since changed. So, I would like you to see the world and make your choices as you see fit." The conversation I had with my mother was the most eye-opening conversation I'd ever had with anyone. My mom opened my room door to let herself out. "One last question before you go, mom," I whispered. My mother stopped in her tracks, "What now," she asked. "Mom, do you think dad would still feel the same hatred towards people of color had you told him the truth?" My mother closed my room door so her answer wouldn't seep past her whisper. "Natalie, it isn't that your dad was lied to. I told him how I felt about Natbo long before he asked me to marry him. At that time, and even to this day, he seems like he's still in competition with my past. Your dad always felt I would fall head over heels for him as I'd fallen for Natbo. Surely, I love FO, but it isn't the same type of love I still have for Natbo.

And lastly, the reason your dad disliked Natbo may have been justified, but his reason for hating all people of color could've been embedded in him long before Natbo or I was even a sparkle in our parents eyes. So, there's nothing anyone can do or say to make him change." My mother kissed me on the cheek, opened my room door for what would be her final exit, and walked away.

"Natalie"

My mom gave me a new perspective on everything. My life, my mindset, and most importantly, my future. I took a shower, and afterwards, I got on my laptop and immediately started looking for apartments somewhere out on the West Coast. I'd heard nothing but great things about Los Angeles, California, so I knew I could do well in that type of environment. I caught a flight out to LA a month later. I'd applied for an apartment online and was instantly approved. I ended up living a few blocks away from McGiver's Law Firm, supposedly the most distinguished law firm in the state of California. I felt good about moving to 'LA. I saw it as a chance to broaden my horizons. I thought I may as well apply for a job at McGiver's Law Firm while things seem to be falling into place step by step. I did apply and was immediately hired. I was asked to start work the following week. I consider myself lucky to have gotten an apartment and a job less than two blocks away from one another in California. Well, I also felt if this was some type of lucky wave flowing through the air, then I wanted to ride it until it stopped.

Natalie

Two Years later

My parents are still trying to tell me how I should live my life. They don't like the fact that I happen to be more open-minded than they are. I really don't think people should be judged by their skin color. I feel my parents are more concerned about my preference for men than anything else. My father was so upset last year when I told him I'd met David, a Black man from Washington, D.C., with whom I was expecting a child. The tone in his voice changed instantly. When I would call to check and see how things were in West Virginia, my dad would be very short on the phone. My friends Nicolette and Tasha of West Virginia called me and told me my dad had a mild heart attack after I told him, months after meeting David, that I was expecting his child. My dad went so far with his hatred; he even banned me and my daughter, Alexis, from ever visiting them in West Virginia. My mother seemed equally upset but didn't go as far as verbalizing she didn't want us to ever visit. I reminded my mother that she had encouraged me to date or marry whomever I chose. She seemed to have forgotten everything she'd encouraged me to do. Perhaps being around my dad seemed to have rubbed off on her in a negative way. She had started to think much like my dad these past two years. I felt they were both inconsiderate and too old-fashioned. So, I made a point my daughter and I just stayed home and watched movies during the holidays instead of visiting my parents. I also made a point to never introduce my daughter to her grandparents. Some folks would think of me as being selfish, but I do not want my daughter to experience or witness the amount of prejudice her grandparents still have for people of color. Sometimes, I find myself wanting to find someone like Edward Keats, our new boss at McGiver's Law Firm. Edward is from Atlanta, Georgia. He seems to have a level head about everything. Edward is smart, handsome, hard-working, and stylish. One of my duties at work is to prepare his Coffee every morning. Shame on me, but I would intentionally drop his stirrer on the floor just so he could reach down and pick it up with hopes he would look directly into my eyes. I just knew he would pick it up. He has been quite a gentleman since the first day he started. I would do other subtle, silly things or drop cute little one-liners just so he would pick up my advances. Although I had this awesome crush on this man, there was one incident that happened where I almost totally lost it. I foolishly complimented him on his cologne. He looked at me and never even said thank you. He made me feel as if I wasn't even standing in front of him. I was so upset I went home and loaded my .38 revolver. I thought to myself that if he ever ignores me again, it would be his last time doing so. It may have been a stupid way of thinking, but that was the type of effect his silence had on me. I've since learned to control my emotions.

Anna B

I was born in Santa Barbara, California. I consider myself to be a private person. I normally don't open up to anyone. As a matter of fact, some folks here in California think that I am anti-social. And I am comfortable with that label. I really don't care what people say or think of me. I've learned when you allow people to know who you are, they feel they should also be able to know your business. So, I don't mingle or have so-called friends over at my place. I keep to myself. I work at McGiver's Law Firm as an executive. Whenever my co-workers or people in general ask me if I am single, I would always say, "No, I'm not. I happen to be married to my money." Oddly, some things have changed ever since our firm hired Edward Keats. Edward seems different. He has a swagger about himself, unlike anyone I've ever met. His work ethic is incredible. He is always diligent about any task the firm asks of him. He takes pride in his work. And, the thing that really impressed me was the firm gave Edward a to-do list that would normally take up to eight or nine months to complete. Edward completed the job in half the amount of time. Another thing that made me start paying attention to Edward even more was that he seemed focused, as if he was on some sort of mission. I wasn't sure what his mission was, but I could sense his diligence would eventually pay off. During our lunch breaks, the entire staff would eat lunch at 'Nathaniel's Café. This eatery makes the best Pastrami sandwiches I've ever tasted. While my co-workers would sit and discuss unimportant, mind-boggling incidents that happened in past relationships, I would use this lunch hour to try to come up with strategies on how I could make McGiver's Law Firm another billion dollars in the coming year so our company could possibly expand internationally. I noticed also that Edward didn't interact with the other co-workers for more than five minutes. I believe this was his way of saying, "My tolerance to nonsense has a time limit." I never told anyone, but I once had a dream that Edward stood in front of a football stadium full of strangers and proposed to me. Oddly, I yelled "Hell No" so loud in my sleep that I thought I might've awakened my neighbors. The crazy thing is, I wanted to apologize to Edward when we met at work the following day, but I'm sure he would've looked at me as if I'd lost my mind. So, I chilled and kept my dream to myself.

Anna B.

I happen to live by a code. That code is, "If it doesn't make dollars, it doesn't make sense." Some folks feel that money isn't everything. That may be very true, but I feel without money, you can't do anything. So, it is safe to say that I am a paper-chaser. Also, some folks may view me as somewhat of a narcissist simply because I don't let people get close to me. That assessment may or may not be accurate. However, one thing is certain. I do like nice things, and I've got high standards. I feel if you can't bring anything to my table, you can't eat. And if I have to feed both of us, you might starve.'

There isn't one person at this law firm, or anywhere in Los Angeles, for that matter, that knows anything about me. I love being mysterious. If anyone asks me a question that isn't job-related, I immediately say to them, " My business shouldn't be your concern." I'm sure I am being looked at as aloof, but I really don't give a damn what others say or think of me.

Chapter Two
Veronica Dubose

Working at McGiver's Law firm with Edward Keats, who happens to be my boss as well as one of my best friends, is actually a blessing. I remember me, Edward, and Marcus playing as kids in Decatur, Georgia. Edward's mom, LaDonna, would bake cookies for us every chance she got. She would always tell us to look out for one another, no matter what. Marcus and Edward were like my big brothers. I was a few years older, so I would give them pointers about how cold-hearted girls can be and what to look out for. They would fight boys who disrespected me in any way. Marcus's mother, Ms. Johnson, was always busy working. So, we would be over at Marcus's house as often as possible. Edward and I would watch Marcus pick his guitar. I was amazed that he taught himself how to play. Edward and I would sit in amazement as Marcus would play *"Frampton Comes Alive"* until we got tired of listening. Edward would display some of his finished Poetry with us. Edward even had a unique way of signing his name on the back of each poem he wrote. He would sign "Ed, the Great" on the back of every one of his pieces. Unique, I thought. My mother Sarah and I lived a few houses down from Marcus and Edward. I'd never met two people so talented and determined as Marcus and Edward. I wanted the same grit and determination so I would hang around them. People always assumed they were my brothers. And we went along with their assumptions. My mother was a nurse's assistant but would eventually become a Registered Nurse, working at the local hospital downtown. My father, Joseph, had provided for her throughout their entire marriage. She started working full-time after my father lost his battle with Cancer in 2017. When my father passed, my mother emphatically instilled in me to always have my own. She would go on further to say, "There may come a time when the person or people you rely on won't be able to do what they'd like to help you, so learn to do for you." I understood where she was coming from. I saw with my own eyes what she'd gone through. Years later, I began working as a waitress downtown Peachtree, five miles from home. It was good money, but I was getting tired of the hustle and bustle of the never-ending traffic stalls on I-285, so I moved out to LA the following spring to make a better life for myself. I went to UCLA, got my Master's Degree, and flirted with an acting career, which didn't work out at all. I met this guy, Reginald Atkins, a semi-pro football player from Michigan, who took my heart away the first year I moved here. He seemed to have wanted the best for me and even introduced me to producers in the acting business, but he wasn't honest. He didn't believe in loyalty. He took me for granted. He felt he could still date multiple women because we weren't married. The crazy thing is, he wasn't ready for marriage, and obviously, neither was I. So, I backed off from seeing him and decided my life and career were much too valuable to be chasing someone that didn't want to be caught.

Veronica

'Two Years Later'

My dad had retired as a Longshoreman, and my mother is currently an RN. So, the idea of failing was not in my family's DNA. Even when I had relationships that didn't seem to work out, I never looked at them as failures. Instead, I labeled them as lessons learned. My parents taught me to be strong and independent. My dad had this cliché he stood by. He would say, 'If you wait for someone to do things for you, you're setting yourself up to fail." That adage made great sense to me. I took it with me everywhere I went, and I made sure I never forgot it. At twenty-three years old, I knew I wanted more to life. I wanted to be successful like my parents. So when I moved to Los Angeles, California, despite not knowing anyone, I was determined to make it big! I waited on tables at several fine dining restaurants while I learned my way around. I stumbled into Reginald Atkins again. We had a long conversation, and it seemed he had grown up since we last talked. Ever since the day we met, I was always attracted to him. I liked the fact that he was articulate with his words, and his broad shoulders could always sweep me off my feet. He was like no one I'd ever dated. He took his time with me. He listened to my horrid stories from past relationships. He showed so much compassion, which, in some way, helped me cope with the pain from my past. With Reginald, I felt I could be myself without having any reservations about anything. One Friday night, I allowed Reginald to have keys to my place, just so I would be able to call on him if I were to lose my own. I've always had a tendency to act somewhat clumsy at times.

Well, my parents taught me never to trust everyone you meet and to be cautious of everything. I've always enjoyed the breeze of the West Coast's winds at night. I would sleep with my windows open just a bit. On this particular Friday night, I heard a sound as if a mouse was trying to enter my apartment. I kept a wooden club by my bedside at all times. When I got up to scare what I thought was a pest, I realized it was not a pest, but someone either trying to pick my lock or searching for the right key to let him or herself in.

Veronica

I grabbed the club from my bedside. I stood behind the door without making a sound. Luckily, it was a full moon on this particular night. The reflection from the moon made it clear to see the subject as he tip-toed towards my bed with a towel in his hands as if he was preparing to suffocate me. I could see it was Reginald. His bulging shoulders were recognizable. Apparently, he realized he'd forgotten to close the door behind him. When he turned to quietly close the door, I slammed my club between his legs as hard as I could. Reginald fell to the floor in excruciating pain. I was taught this technique by Marcus and Edward while growing up in Atlanta. Although it was my first time having to use it, I made sure I didn't miss my target. As Reginald lay in pain, I thought it would be best to call the Los Angeles Police Department. I dialed 911, and within minutes, they were there to arrest Reginald. I didn't want my mother to know what had happened, because I'd spoken so highly of Reginald in the past. Surely, she would worry herself to death if she found out what had happened. So, I thought it would be best she not know. I did, however, tried calling my brothers, Marcus and Edward, to let them know what had happened. Edward lived in LA, and we worked together at the firm, but I hardly heard from him away from work due to his many business investments. And Marcus, according to circulating rumors from my folks back in Atlanta, was working on an interesting project. I wanted to thank them both for the lessons of self-defense they'd taught me. I learned on that particular Friday night that Reginald also had a history of molesting women. Police had warrants out for his arrest dating back ten years. It taught me a valuable lesson indeed. In the famous words of my brother, Marcus, "You can never fully trust anyone."

Veronica

I never understood why Reginald changed. Or, maybe he didn't change at all. Perhaps it was me being blinded by his bulging shoulders that caused the oversight. Reginald ended up getting a ten-year prison sentence. I was in attendance during his trial. A part of me felt it was my fault he got caught. But the other part of me still wonders what Reginald's intent was on that breezy Friday night. I guess I would never know. I can only assume whatever his intent was, it couldn't have been good.

I finally got a return phone call from my brother, Marcus. I filled him in on everything that had transpired over the course of several months, that he went MIA. When Marcus heard what Reginald tried to do to me, he immediately suggested that I get a firearm for protection. Initially, Marcus was upset at me for allowing Reginald to get so close to me. But I had to remind Marcus that I no longer had him or Edward to lean on like in years past. And even though I was certain they would be at my rescue at any given moment, neither one of them was close enough to rescue me if that should ever happen again. Edward and I lived in the same city and worked at the same job, but we only saw each other at work or in passing. Edward was busy most times. I understood that his life had changed, and although I knew our friendship would always be there, I also knew his career and vast businesses would be his main focus. So, the following week, I went out and purchased a .38 Smith and Wesson Revolver. I went to the shooting range for six straight weeks so I would be able to handle myself comfortably if another situation occurs. My firearm instructor, Tommy, assumed I'd taken firearms lessons before. I'm sure he made that assumption based on my accuracy at the gun range. Within a few days, I was hitting my target with precision. More importantly, I felt safe and secure. I learned a lot from my ordeal with Reginald. I now understand why you should never assume everyone has your best interest at heart.

Chapter Three
Rosalind Butler

I am originally from Gary, Indiana, home of the late great Michael Jackson and the Jackson 5's. I am proud to have graduated from Harvard University. I graduated as the 'Top Student' of my class. I work here at McGiver's Law Firm, where I have to sit back and watch as employees come in less educated and get paid more. I feel I've put in the time and dedication to be a partner in this company. Of course, the firm pays well, but obviously, the pay is substantially greater when you become a partner. I am somewhat bitter because they've always seemed to ignore the fact that I've paid my dues. Sometimes, I get so outraged at the way they show favoritism towards Edward Keats, but when it comes to me, they act as if I'm just someone they can overlook. Yes, I am bitter. I am a single parent. I've got a daughter, Ashley, who has just started kindergarten. Ashley's father, Curtis, doesn't support her. I told him from day one I didn't need his help financially, but it would mean a lot if he would come by, pick his daughter up, and take her places when I needed a break. He said he would but has never once been true to his word. When it comes to his own daughter, he seems to choose his wife's kid over his own. The night Curtis and I slept together, he lied to me and told me he was single. It wasn't until after I got pregnant he came forward and told me he was married. I told him I wouldn't have slept with him had I known the truth. Just so I wouldn't ruin his marriage, I decided to take care of my kid myself. But raising a kid alone is way tougher than I thought. To say I am bitter is an understatement. I am sick and tired of everyone. My daughter's father, my landlord, Ms.Teresa, who keeps raising the rent every year, it seems, and all of my co-workers here at the firm. They all act like their shit doesn't stink, especially Anna B. and Edward. They get the best of everything. They both have the best office views at work, the high profile cases, and all of the employee in-house awards. Edward gets to drive around in a company 'Porsche'. I don't feel he's been with the company long enough to be getting the royal treatment he's been awarded. Yet, they praise him as if he's some type of God. I am at a place where my stomach aches the moment I get to work. I open my drawer each morning and look at my pearl-white handle .38 revolver with evil intent. I think about these so-called sophisticated co-workers I've got to deal with every single day; I think about how selfish Curtis is with his own daughter; and I look at how he lives selfishly every single day of his life, and I think to myself, should this be the day I end it all with one pull of the trigger. But something made me think twice, and I decided to live at least one more day. Meanwhile, I plan to stay with this company for just one more year, but if anyone irks my nerves before then, it will become a problem. PERIOD. I am an educated woman. But sometimes, folks take me for granted. They don't understand I can go from nice to nasty in a New York minute.

Rosalind

The firm knows how I feel. I express my unhappiness every chance I get. They seem to ignore my complaints. But one day, I'm going to come to work with my handgun and just start firing at everyone. I do believe Anna B. would be the first I go after. She doesn't believe her shit stinks at all. She takes her monthly trips to Dubai, and since Edward started working here, she really believes she lives beyond the clouds. To sum it up bluntly, I really don't like any of my co-workers, to be quite honest. If the job didn't pay so well, I would've been gone a long time ago.

Tammy Richardson

I hail from Bethlehem, Pennsylvania. I am a huge Pittsburgh Steelers fan. I moved to LA because I wanted to experience the West Coast. I wanted to live in an environment with some of Hollywood's finest actors and actresses alike. My parents are from Dayton, Ohio. They never got to travel or see much of anywhere else in this wonderful world, so I didn't want my life to be similar to theirs. My dad is a retired railroad operator, and my mother is a former High School Science teacher. They agreed that when I was done with college, they would relocate to someplace quiet and remote. I was a good kid, according to my parents. I was an only child. When I reached the age of twelve, my dad taught me self-defense. He would take me to our backyard, where he had hung a 200-pound punching bag from an Oak Tree limb. He showed me what I should do if I were ever attacked from behind, how to counter someone if they were to swing at me and missed, and how to fight off men who were a lot bigger and stronger than me. My father called it 'molding me for the future.' I am only 5'3. Because of my small stature, my dad thinks people would try to take advantage of me. So he thought he would prepare me to be able to handle myself if a situation were to arise. My dad was tough as nails. I was told by my neighbors, Michelle and Mona, that when I was about five years old, my mother, Christina, bought me a one-year-old German Shepherd. I named my puppy "King". It is said that I was playing by a nearby lake one afternoon when 'King' was attacked by an 8 ft. Alligator. The neighbors recalled in order for my dad to save my pup, he ended up grabbing the alligator by its tail and tossing it halfway across the lake. Rumor also has it that is where my dad's nickname, "Toss em," originated .

Tammy

I went to the University of Maryland. I happen to be a proud terrapin through and through. While at college, I met Lashanda Sanchez, a gorgeous young woman from Amazonas, Brazil. She had some of the most amazing physical features I'd ever seen. Her lips were perfect, her eyes were olive green, her skin was dark, and her body was so chiseled that it seemed as if she'd been eating nothing but grass her entire life. For short, I called her '*LS*'. In college, we all shortened each other's names. It was the trending thing. Much the same as I shortened her name, she would call me 'TR'. She knew I was attracted to her, but she didn't look at me any differently. I believe she'd grown so accustomed to people of all types being attracted to her that she knew how to handle situations without hurting anyone's feelings. 'LS' pulled me to the side one day. She said, "Listen up, 'TR'. I know what you're feeling. I could be wrong, but I've been around you enough to feel confident in what I'm about to say. You have this attraction for me, I know. Just so you and I would have a clear understanding, you and I could never be more than friends. I have an attraction for the opposite sex, despite the ones I had to walk away from were all losers. My preference is like working at the Post Office. It's "Male all day, every day." I couldn't help but laugh at LS's comments. After our conversation, 'LS' leaned over, kissed me on my forehead, and said, "You shouldn't have any problems getting anyone you want; just make sure the ones you go after are worth your time and positive energy." Those words meant a lot coming from someone like her. She had everything; Brains, Beauty, Body, and an amazing personality. 'LS' went on to become 'Miss

Maryland' six months later. I felt the award was well deserved. And, it gave me chills to know the award was presented to such a wonderful person and friend. After we graduated, LS' moved to Vermont and met Marino, a Tomato farmer, and they are now married with twin daughters, Katie and Kendra. The pointers 'LS' gave me about making sure the one I go after is deserving stuck with me to this day. I've learned to be patient. I don't go out looking for anyone in particular. If the person meant for me is alive, I'm certain we will eventually meet.

Tammy

LA' is a happening city. As I reflect back, I remember soon after getting my Master's Degree, I was fortunate to run into Joe Emory, CEO and hiring agent for McGivers Law Firm. While grocery shopping, we said hello but didn't know each other at all. After I'd done my shopping, I was carrying my bags to my car, and one of the bottles of wine I'd just purchased happened to fall out and shatter. I recall Joe running over to help, but it was too late. "Sorry I couldn't catch it in time, but if you'd like, I would gladly purchase another bottle for you," explained Joe. "No, that's okay. I probably didn't need it anyway," I said. Joe insisted I take him up on his offer. Well, I thought about it. He looked to be in his eighties, so I didn't think he had a hidden agenda. So I took him up on the bottle of Chardonnay. We struck up a conversation, and he explained who he was and that his company was in need of a good secretary. Joe and I exchanged telephone numbers. The following week, he called me up and asked if I could start work immediately. "Yes, of course," I replied. I was elated to be hired by the largest law firm in the state of California. I called my parents and let them know I finally got a job. But, not just any job. I told my parents if any of my friends back home were to ask, tell them I am currently working as secretary for the largest Law firm in the state of California.

Herman Yanez

(Anna B.'s son)

I reside in Oakland, California. I am my mother's only child. I never got a chance to know my biological father for reasons unknown. Whenever I would ask my mother about my father, she would always say, "Your father doesn't exist." I've always wondered if he died or was it my mother's way of saying he wasn't a part of our lives. I never had a father figure growing up, so when I turned sixteen years old, I joined a gang called "The Heart Stoppers." I imagine my mother did the best she could in trying to raise me on her own, but I feel life would've been better if we had a father figure in our household. But I also understood life doesn't always provide us with what we want. "Heart Stoppers" was a non-violent group consisting of mostly teens that grew up in poverty-stricken neighborhoods. The group was led by Darren D, an intelligent brother who was raised by his grandfather. He, like myself and many other teens in the group, never got to know our biological fathers for different reasons. But fortunately for Darren D, his grandfather was more than just a grandfather; he became Darren D's mentor and father figure. He was knowledgeable about everything. He was a former High School Principal, spoke five different languages fluently, and, most importantly, he took time out with Darren D to instill in him how to be a man and how to take accountability for his actions.

Herman

Darren D' took those valuable qualities his grandfather instilled in him and tried to instill them in members of our gang. For those of us who needed assistance with school work, Darren D' took time out to help. Not only would he assist us with our homework, he would break down each equation and show us how he came up with the answers for each. I remember, as a kid, I loved basketball. I told my mom I wanted to become a basketball star one day. Even though she never took the time to see me play, she went out and bought me a basketball so I could hone my skills. I practiced a lot at the local Rec Center. I got good at it. The JV basketball coach, Elton Grover, stopped by to see me play one afternoon. He apparently liked the way I played. Afterward, he asked me to check with my mom to see if it would be okay if I could come out to play for his team. I went home and asked my mom that evening if I could join the JV's basketball squad. My mom looked me in the eye and responded, "No, you won't be joining Elton's JV basketball team." I was so disappointed. I realized at that very moment how selfish my mother was. Her reasoning for not allowing me to join the team was; "she didn't want folks poking fun at me if I didn't play well." It was the most idiotic reason I'd ever heard. Her reasoning was what changed my mindset about her as a person. I started to pay attention to her every move. She would stay out and won't return until the following day. Of course, she was single, so I imagined she could do whatever she wanted. But I had a problem with her never calling home to check to see if I was okay. Her selfishness was what caused me to join 'Heart Stoppers' in the first place."

Herman

I was considered by many to be a smart kid in school. I made the Honor Roll every single year. Also, I made straight A's throughout the school year. I was looked up to and respected by my peers. Everyone thought my mom was the reason I kept my grades up, but my mom hardly asked me about homework or what my schoolwork consisted of. She happened to peek at my report card one afternoon and was amazed at how well I'd done. "Where did you learn about Algebra and Biology, son?" she asked. I didn't want her to know I was being mentored and taught by a gang leader, so I lied to her and told her I was taught by my peers at the local Rec Center.

It was June 3, High School Graduation Day. For me, it was the biggest day of my young life. I kept looking in the audience for my mom but she never showed up. I was devastated. I didn't know what had happened. My peers kept asking me about my mom's whereabouts, but I had no answer. So, I decided to tell folks who would ask, "My mother got sick on the way to my graduation." It was a lie I had to remember for the rest of my life. I love my mother dearly, but she happens to be one of the most selfish adults I've ever been around. She only cares about money and what matters to her. So, after my graduation, I moved to Oakland, California. I decided to lease a cozy, Two-Bedroom Apartment. I use one of my bedrooms as a Tattoo Parlor. Painting and Writing were two of the things Darren D taught us, in addition to so many other great things. I've become one of the best Tattoo artists in all of Oakland. I make a decent living at it. I never had to ask my mother for anything.

Even though she wasn't the best mom, I would still do anything in the world for her.

Herman

My mother doesn't seem to understand how much I love her. Despite not being in attendance during my graduation, I didn't hold it against her. Or should I say I didn't hold it against her forever. Her explanation as to what actually happened pissed me off more than anything. "I'd forgotten your special day, son. But I will make it up to you," she'd say to me days later. What bothered me the most was I happened to stumble across a video of my mom and some guy named Derrick, dancing together in Jamaica on the internet the night of my graduation. I never once mentioned this to my mom.. She didn't lie to me about where she was, she told me she'd forgotten when my graduation was. When I thought about it, she may have been telling the truth about forgetting my special day, but what kind of person would forget their only child's graduation? As time passed, I finally told a few of my peers in my gang the truth about my mom's whereabouts during my graduation. They even thought it was an awful excuse. "Only a selfish person could've done such a thing," they'd tell me. I eventually got over it. But one brother in my gang, Gino Sanchez, took matters into his own hands to research the guy my mom danced with the night of my graduation. He found the guy's number and told me he'd contacted him, and he knew his exact whereabouts. Gino informed me the guy was living nearby in San Fransisco, California. It didn't matter to me who the guy was, but Gino must've understood the hurt I'd felt that night my mother didn't attend my graduation. I'm not even sure what type of relationship, if any, my mother had with this guy, nor did I care. But Gino saw things differently.

Herman

'A Month Later'

I got a surprise call from Gino early one Friday morning. Gino told me I no longer had to worry about my mother's friend ever again. I was like, "What do you mean?"I made him disappear," said Gino. "I hope you didn't kill the guy," I said. I got no response. All I heard for the next few seconds was a dial tone. I called my mom immediately to see if she was okay. I wanted to ask her if anything had gone wrong with any of her friends, but I realized it would've seemed awfully suspicious to ask about folks I'd never asked about before. I figured if anything bad had happened to any of her friends, I didn't want her to think I may have attributed in some way. So I just chilled. About an hour later, my mom called me to tell me she'd lost a friend. I asked her who was her friend and how close of a friendship did they have. "Just a guy I met back in June. His name was Derrick," she mumbled. I offered my condolences and told her if there was anything I could do, let me know. By the tone of my mom's voice, their relationship wasn't worth someone dying over. I was too afraid to ask my mom what happened to her friend because I didn't want my guilty conscience to somehow be detected through the phone line. So I let her cry on the phone while I held the phone for as long as I thought she needed me to. Simply knowing I was on the other end seemed to have given her comfort. When she was finally done crying, she said, "Thank you for being there, son. Goodbye, and we shall talk soon." Never once did she ask me if I was okay. But that is how my mom is. She won't ever change.

Every so often, I wonder what my mother would think if she actually found out I attributed indirectly to her friend's death. I also wonder if she knows I inherited some of those selfish ways she has. The truth of the matter is I never did like another man coming into my mother's life. Anytime I felt she was interested in some guy, I wouldn't talk to her for months. I guess I am somewhat territorial. I know I shouldn't say this, but I would probably kill anyone that gets close to my mom. It is a selfish way to think, but it is the side of my mother I had inherited. Just so she won't see that ugly side of me, I rarely visit her!

Edward Keats

When I was a kid, I watched my mother, LaDonna, work diligently at low-paying jobs to make sure I was taken care of. After the death of my father, Edward Sr., who was killed in an automobile accident on I-285 a few years ago, she became overly protective of me. It seemed as if my well-being was the only thing that mattered to her in this world. My mother didn't have a lot of friends. She was more of an introvert. She never let a day go by without telling me she loves me. When I got older, I decided to ask my mother what makes her tell me she loves me every single day. My mother sat me down and said, "Son, I learned a valuable lesson when your father died. I never once told him I loved him. At the time, I guess it was my silly way of not allowing him to know how much of my heart he actually had. I can still hear him jokingly saying to me, "Don't you wait until I'm dead to give me flowers." On the night of his automobile accident, I bought a dozen roses, went by the hospital, held his hand, and told him I loved him for the first time. Even though every bone in his face was shattered, he tried everything he could to smile. I felt if his smile could speak, it would've said, "You almost didn't make it in time with my flowers, dear." He died two minutes after I gave him those flowers. So from that day moving forward, I decided to never take even one second for granted ever again." My mother seemed to have explained herself quite clearly. I now fully understand why she reminds me constantly that she loves me.

I wanted to do something for my mother that would make her proud. Atlanta was a great spot for fun, but it wasn't the city I had the vision of being successful in. I called my best friend, Marcus, and asked him if he could join me for dinner. A few hours later, Marcus came over. We ate steamed Lobster, Beef Tenderloin, mixed vegetables, and Baked Potatoes. Afterward, we discussed what would be best for our mothers. I shared with Marcus that having a bachelor's degree from Emory University was all fine, but it wasn't bringing in a six-figure income. Sometimes, I felt I should've chosen another career because finding a good job in Atlanta was not working in my favor. I told Marcus I was thinking about moving out to Los Angeles, California. Marcus mentioned how his career as a musician was just enough to keep food on the table for him and his mother, but it wasn't his definition of being successful either. He assured me he had a better plan in store. We both decided that whichever paths we chose, we would have each other's back if needed. However, our main goal was always to make sure our mothers wouldn't have to work ever again.

Edward

'The Following Day'

Yesterday, Marcus and I discussed the idea of one day placing our mothers together at an elite retirement facility. We also shared a laugh or two about the time we were in our teens, approximately sixteen or seventeen years old, when I got so upset at Marcus because he had stolen a girlfriend of mine. So, while we were eating our meal, Marcus thought he would apologize to me again several years later, for what he called a mishap back then. He and I laughed so hard when I told him that I was upset at him for that entire year because of that incident. Marcus and I laughed even harder when we realized neither of us could remember what the girl's actual name was. Marcus and I had a bond like no other. I've always thought it was God's way of placing a brother in my corner I never had. We both had always been interested in music and arts. Although Marcus was a much better musician than I ever dreamed to be, I was the self-proclaimed Poet. Marcus and my mother would always say to me, "Poetry is God's gift to you." I was a big fan of Edgar Allan Poe's. I remember writing poems, and afterward, I would show them off to Marcus, my mother, and Veronica, the oldest girl in the neighborhood, for which Marcus and I looked at as our big sister. After discussing my plan with Marcus on yesterday, we gave each other a hug and a fist bump and wished each other well.

I wasn't sure what Marcus's plan was, but I knew he was smart, and whatever he decided on becoming, it would be for the benefit of his mom. So, I didn't worry about him at all. I packed my belongings and spoke to my mother extensively about moving out to LA with me. My mother never cared much about the West Coast. She has always said, "Too much smog out that way for me." It's funny when I think about it. I told my mom I would register her into the best retirement facility Atlanta has to offer and that I would make sure she has everything she'd ever need at her disposal. My mother had the brightest smile I'd ever seen. She always wanted the best for me. And I'd promised myself that I would provide the best for her whenever I was able to. I'd saved up a good nest egg over the years. I was able to get her registered into *Buck-Head Retirement Center*, the best retirement facility in the Atlanta area, and I still had plenty enough cash left for my move to the West Coast. My mother fell in love with the place the moment she saw it. During her first week at her new place, she and I ate lunch together every day at 12.00 p.m., sharp. This facility's logo on the door was perfect. It read, "A Suite for the Sweetest." The following week, it was time for me to head out to 'LA'. My mother kissed me goodbye and said, "Be careful and always check on Marcus." I caught the two o'clock flight from Hartsfield, and off to Los Angeles I went.

Edward

The moment I arrived in California, I was in awe of the city, its bright lights, and how diverse it seemed. I was able to flag down a taxi cab instantly. The Taxi driver, Abayomi, told me he was from Nigeria and he'd lived in LA for the past twenty years. He seemed knowledgeable about everything. I noticed California's rush hour traffic reminded me of Atlanta's at 5.00 p.m., with the only exception; California has a lot more lanes. While we crept along at three miles per hour, I was totally shocked at the many homeless people I saw living under bridges, side roads, and sidewalks. Even though I'd seen homeless people in the streets of Atlanta, I'd never seen it at this magnitude. On my first day in LA, I experienced an eye-opening surprise I had never imagined. Even though I was a bit disheartened, I had to stay mentally focused on anything out of the ordinary from this day moving forward. I remember using my phone app to confirm that my apartment would be ready by the time I got there. After I'd gotten my confirmation, Abayomi started filling me in on everything from where the hottest beaches were to where not to go. He told me about the wildfires that could possibly be coming towards the neighborhood I am currently moving into in less than a week. "The south side of LA is supposed to be lit up by next week," explained Abayomi. "Well, we would just have to wait and see, my brother," I calmly replied. He and I talked about everything, it seemed. Also, his knowledge of the city, the hottest spots, best restaurants, and where the best Jazz Bars were was evident I'd chosen the right driver. An odd moment occurred when he looked me in the eye and said, "Brother, please don't forget to pray. I foresee dark clouds ahead." I've always believed in prayer, but this was a bright, sunny day when I arrived in LA. So I looked at my driver like, 'what in the world he sees that I cannot?" But the look in his eyes told me this could be a premonition or a message coming from a higher power. This message would stick with me for as long as I could remember.

I realized we'd been talking for almost three hours already, but it felt like we hadn't moved an inch. Finally, traffic started to move faster. Although I was somewhat exhausted, it seemed my conversation with my driver helped restore my energy level tremendously. We finally arrived at my apartment. I paid my fare and thanked Abayomi for the valuable information he'd shared.

Edward

'First Two Weeks in New Apartment'

I moved into, *The Breakers,* a modest, two-bedroom apartment with hardwood floors and high ceilings. It had all the amenities I wanted and needed. I was comfortable with everything about the place. I lived less than a quarter mile from a grocery store, a movie theater was across the street, a fitness center sat in the shopping center across from a bookstore, and a coffee shop was approximately two blocks down. Everything seemed so right.

During my first two weeks in LA, I made it a point to get to know my neighbors as well as my neighborhood. My first chat was with my neighbors, Willie Mae and John, a beautiful couple originally from Hilton Head Island, S.C., who had moved to LA a few years earlier. They both were kind and well-groomed. The perfect couple, I thought. After hours of seemingly small talk about military aircraft, John finally grasped my attention when he mentioned about this great church across town he and Willie Mae thought I would like to attend. A good church to visit and eventually join was definitely on my priority list. So, the following Sunday, I decided to catch the city bus to visit this church. It was nestled in a very nice neighborhood. The pastor, Reverend Delaney, preached an amazing service. After church service, while walking to the bus stop to head back home, I noticed a Library across the street that stayed open all day. Much to my surprise, it served hot coffee and Donuts until eight O'clock. I felt like I had stumbled into Heaven by moving to LA. Despite the many good fortunes I've been experiencing in such a short time, I started to think of my mother and Marcus back home. I wondered what they would think of this library if they got to see it. I was getting somewhat concerned about my mother because I hadn't been able to chat with her for the past two weeks. I wasn't overly concerned about Marcus because I knew he could handle himself well in any situation, but I'd been trying to contact him several times but was not able to do so.

Edward

'A few Weeks Later'

I finally got a return call from Vanessa, my mother's nurse from the retirement facility. Vanessa assured me that my mother was doing well and that she'd been sleeping comfortably of late. She also assured me that she would have my mother call me as soon as the opportunity is presented. A few days later, my mother did call to let me know she was resting peacefully and reassured me Marcus was doing well and had just visited her earlier in the day.

My mind was at peace knowing the two most important people in my life were okay. The following day, I concentrated solely on my new job at McGiver's Law Group. I never thought I would get a job at such a prestigious law firm. Hell, I still can't believe I got hired by the first place I sent my resume to. I could hardly wait to tell Marcus I am employed by the most distinguished law firm in California. I feel honored and blessed to have been hired by this law group.

Edward

On my first day on the job, I was welcomed by CEO and hiring agent Joe Emory. He told me he had read my resume thoroughly. He walked me through the office to meet my new co-workers with whom I would be working alongside. "These co-workers are under your jurisdiction from this day moving forward. They all know what needs to be done, but your job is to make sure they do their job in a professional and timely manner. If you have no questions, I would like to proceed with my introduction," said Joe. " I have no questions at all," I replied. Joe opened the first office door. "This is Tammy Richardson, a young, intelligent, and well-spoken secretary from Pennsylvania. She happens to be a very proud University of Maryland, graduate. I shook Tammy's hand and told her it would be a pleasure working with her. "The feeling is mutual, sir," said Tammy. Next, he introduced me to Anna B., a business executive from Santa Barbara, California. Joe informed me that the firm sends Anna B. to Dubai monthly to better the firm's relationship with international bigwigs for future trade dealings. Joe turned to me and whispered, "Anna B. isn't one to carry long conversations with anyone. She is strictly about her work." I shook Anna B.'s hand and said, " I promise I won't get in your way." Her response was, "I will make certain to hold you to that promise." Joe looked at me and smiled as we exited to the next office. Joe then opened the door to the office, where the name *Natalie* hung in bold letters. Joe said, "This is Natalie Owens, a talented young woman from West Virginia. She can be somewhat edgy at times, but her office skills are incredible." After walking away from Natalie's office, Joe mentioned Natalie has an interesting story. I asked, "Would you care to elaborate?" Joe seemed to have regretted his comment. He replied hesitantly, "Natalie's story is one worthy of being a bestseller, but I would rather her share her own story if she so chooses." Fair enough," I replied. Joe took me across the hallway, opened the door, smiled, and said, " This, of course, is Veronica DuBose. I am quite aware you two know each other. Veronica has told everyone in this office you two grew up together in Atlanta, Georgia." I hugged my sister so tightly and told her how much I'd missed her. "I'd like to move on as soon as possible, Edward," said Joe. We walked over to another door, which was partly ajar. Strangely, I noticed Joe's demeanor changed immediately. He was blunt. He only said three words; "This is Rosalind." Then he immediately backed away. Rosalind turned her head as if she didn't care to hear anything Joe had to say. I instantly detected these two didn't get along very well. So, I shook Rosalind's hand and decided I would ease the tension by complimenting Rosalind on her framed poem, *"Just So You'd Know,"* which was hanging on the wall directly behind her. Because of the depth of the poem, I asked Rosalind if she knew the author personally. Rosalind's response was, "I do not, Sir, but the gentleman hails from South Carolina. We happened to stumble into one another while I was on vacation there. He was reciting this poem in front of an audience of ten beach-goers, and his words drew me in to listen closer. Afterward, I told him how much I loved the poem. Upon leaving, he had it framed and gave it to me as a gift. I thought it was a good gesture, Sir." Indeed it was, I replied. I will look on the internet later to see if this author has any other material out there. I, too, am a fan of his Poetry already. Thanks for sharing," Rosalind.

"Just So You'd Know"

I would like to take a moment to reveal why I still love you the way I do and why I feel there's a higher level you and I could one day reach. This goes back to the very first time I saw you and holds true to this very day. From the moment our eyes connected, your presence seemed angelic, as if you'd just fallen feet-first from Heaven. Your smile was the most beautiful smile I'd ever seen in my lifetime. You, my love, were as beautiful as church music on Easter Sunday. Your lips were as sweet as cotton candy and equally as soft as miniature marshmallows. When you wrapped your arms around me, the warmth from your embrace lit a fire in me that still burns to this day. You've always had this wonderful glow about you. It seemed as if I could clearly see my future in your glow's reflection. Everything about you seemed perfect. But something happened. Or should I say 'life happened'. You did what you thought was best. You went away, and while you were away, you stumbled into someone else who saw you just as I did. So, he did what he thought was best; He claimed you as his very own.. Fate would have you and I reconnect years later. You seem to believe it was pure coincidence, but I always knew we would meet again. I am surprised, however, that our chemistry is still as hot today as it was on that summer evening when we first met. Even though years have come and gone, I still can't seem to get out of my mind how your presence immediately captivated me and left this profound impact on my imagination; I first got to imagine us together in Frankfurt, Germany, where we got to hold hands, snuggle by campfire, and even shared a bowl of Goulash out of the same dish. But then, I was blown away a second time when my imagination had us sitting side by side on the doorsteps of Heaven. You and I were in the presence of a dozen Angels; I was trying to explain to them the very moment you swept me off my feet when all of a sudden, a powerful voice said unto me, "I made both of you perfect for each other, my son. See, I know your hearts better than anyone. So, I designed it so that, when you see her for the first time, she will take your breath away; when she leans forward and presses her lips against yours, she will leave such an impression the mentioning of her name will make your heart smile every day for the rest of your life; Whenever she thinks about you, she will reminisce all those fun-filled moments you shared; Those memories will give her an inner peace and an ultra-bright radiance to her smile; She will then realize no other person on Earth has ever left such an impression on her the way you have; And lastly, she will not only become your inspiration, but also the reason you'd be able to reach new heights." Immediately after that confirmation, I started to reflect back on those times when you reiterated over and over again that I was the one guy who was able to romantically elevate you to altitudes you didn't think were possible. Well, just so you know, there's no limit to how much higher or farther we could go.

Edward

After Joe had introduced me to everyone, he compiled a to-do list for me. It was stacks of back-logged cases that were months behind schedule. I read over each case thoroughly the following week. Within three months, I'd broken down each case and had placed a timetable and agenda sheet so each case would be dealt with in an orderly manner. Joe went over my work the following week. He then sent me an email to let me know he was very satisfied with what I'd done and the timely manner in which I completed the list. Five days later, Joe called a staff meeting. During the meeting, he surprised me with a promotion and a three percent partnership in his company. The following month, I was issued a company car. But not just any car; a brand new Porshe sat in a parking space with a sign that read *"EDWARD'S PARKING SPACE."* The firm threw a party for me at Nathaniel's, an elegant Bistro across the street from the firm's office. This place is where most, if not all, of my co-workers eat for lunch. Everyone in the office came out. All with the exception of Rosalind Butler. I was told she'd informed Joe early on that she wouldn't be available. While everyone seemed to be enjoying themselves, I noticed Anna B. kept to herself. I vaguely remember Joe did say she is someone who doesn't waste time on small talk. But I wanted to get to know Anna B. better. I liked the fact that she was very private. So, I walked over to her while everyone else was laughing and having a good time. I started with petty talk. Then, more petty talk. Finally, she smiled. It was such a gorgeous smile. Her smile alone told me she could be the driving force for which my future could be built around.

Edward

(Anna B. and I)

The fact that Anna B. seemed so private intrigued me. About a week later, I sent her an email and asked if I could have a conversation with her in a private setting. We agreed to meet for lunch at *"Dolan's*, a gourmet sandwich shop at the corner of Shari and Sunset Boulevard. This would become our meeting place for eight consecutive weeks. After two months of finding out each other's likes, dislikes, and everything else in between, I felt this was the woman for me. Over several conversations, we'd established that not only were we compatible, but we could do well together. Although I didn't have any children of my own, I liked how highly Anna B. spoke of her only son, Herman, who lives in Oakland, California but never visits. Anna B. seemed anxious that I meet her son as if I needed his approval or she needed his assessment of me before she and I could become an item.. I didn't have a problem meeting with him, I just didn't know if the timing would interfere with my work schedule. Meanwhile, Anna B. and I had become inseparable. Even though she was a private person, she knew a lot of high-profile people. She showed me around the city, took me to Hollywood, and introduced me to a few entertainers as well as Hollywood celebs. I called my mother to let her know I may found someone that I may want to marry. My mother didn't seem surprised at all. Her only reply was, "I can hardly wait to meet her." I found my mother's response to be awfully funny because I knew for a fact she wasn't ever coming to LA. She told me several times before how much she dislikes the West Coast. She'd always say, "Way too much fog." I tried calling Marcus to fill him in on everything that's been going on, but Marcus was still not available for calls. Although my mother told me he had been visiting her often, and she'd told him how fortunate I've been since moving to LA., I haven't been able to reach him. I did reach out to Veronica, me and Marcus's childhood sister, to inform her of all the great things that has been going on with me and Anna B. the past few months. Veronica was always cool. Her mindset has always been, 'If you're happy, then I am happy for you.'

Edward

'Meeting Herman'

Before Anna B. and I could become one, she told me I needed to meet her son, Herman. We planned a weekend trip to Oakland. Anna B. had arranged that we meet up with her son at *Giovanni's,* an Italian restaurant in downtown Oakland. I am not a fan of Italian food at all, but this was supposed to be a meeting, so I went along with Anna'B's decision to meet there. As soon as we walked into the restaurant, Anna B. screamed, "Herman, oh Herman, I miss you so much." She was awfully excited, but Herman seemed rather nonchalant. It seemed Herman either had some bad spaghetti before we got there, or, he wasn't very happy to see me. I introduced myself and told Herman I'd heard so many great things about him. He did give me a handshake, but it was an unusual handshake. It was more like a hard fist bump. I thought for a split second he might've been trying to break my knuckles. But then I thought again, this might be the way the younger crowd greets nowadays. The artwork on Herman's arms told me he was either in some type of Gang or heavily into tattoos. After about fifteen minutes of watching mother and son try to catch up on family matters, I realized Anna B. had a lot of catching up to do with her son. So, I told them I would excuse myself to catch some fresh air. I walked away and sat in the car until Anna B. was done chatting with Herman. Forty-five minutes later, Anna B. and Herman were exiting the restaurant. I got out of the car to rush over so I could say goodbye to Herman, but he gave me a half-hearted wave and went about his business. When Anna B. got back in the car, I asked, " How did the meeting go?" It was so good to see him," she replied. She then asked, "What did you think of my son?" Just so my reply wouldn't cause an argument, I said," It's kinda hard to judge anyone based on a simple fist-bump. But it was nice to have met your son." I am so glad you met him also," said Anna B.

Edward

'The Proposal'

Before heading back to Los Angeles, Anna B. and I decided to drive around the old Oakland raiders' Coliseum. While driving on Interstate 880, Anna B. told me whenever we do decide to get married, Herman won't be attending our wedding. "I gathered that from the fist bump he gave me," I replied. I thought about asking Anna B. why he won't be attending, but I'm not so sure if I'd want him to anyhow. "It doesn't matter to me one way or the other, hun. I just wanted my son to know that I've found the man I would like to spend the rest of my life with," said Anna B. Those words melted my heart. I took the next exit. As soon as we got off the ramp, I spotted a church. I drove in front of the church and asked Anna B. to step out of the car. "Hun, where are we?" she asked. I told her I needed to stretch my legs. I grabbed Anna B.'s hand and walked to the steps of this roadside church, knelt down, and asked her if she would marry me. "Oh hun, Yes, of course," she replied. I will pick up a ring for you as soon as we get back home," I said. Anna B. couldn't stop crying. "I've got to get home and plan the wedding," said Anna B. Well, I thought a small gathering would be appropriate, being her only son won't be attending, and I haven't been able to touch bases with my best friend, Marcus, for awhile now. So I wrapped my arms around her and whispered, "I think we should just have a nice reception after our honeymoon, my love," Anna B. stopped crying and paused for a brief moment. Much to my surprise, she agreed."Great idea, hun," she replied.

Edward

"Three Hours later"

As soon as we got back from Oakland, I dropped Anna B. off at her apartment and headed downtown to Patty Norman's Jewelry store to seek the most gorgeous diamond ring for my bride-to-be. I knew everything about Anna B., including her finger size. I was also aware of how much she loved Emeralds.. So, I saw the perfect diamond ring Anna B. would love. It was a half-carat diamond ring with an Emerald on each side. I purchased the ring and tipped the jeweler an extra two hundred dollars to gift-wrap it expeditiously. When he was done, I thanked him for everything he'd done, shook his hand, and headed out the door. About an hour later, I called Anna B. and told her I was about to bring her ring over. "Hurry, sweetheart, my Pastor is coming over to speak with us," said Anna B. I sped over to Anna B.'s place as fast as I could. Unlike our meeting with her son, where Anna B. seemed to have forgotten to introduce me altogether, this meeting was different. As soon as I got to Anna B's apartment, Anna B. embraced me and said, "Sweetheart, I would like you to meet Reverend Williams, my Pastor. 'Rev,' this is the love of my life, Edward Keats," said Anna. I shook the Pastor's hand. He held my hand tightly and said to me, "Edward, our meeting is rather spontaneous. I don't usually do weddings on such short notice, but this time, and this time only, I am making an exception." I was shocked because I'd mentioned to Anna B. a wedding wouldn't be necessary, but it seems she's made this decision on her own. With absolutely not one single guest, Anna B. and I were married in less than an hour. I immediately called my mother to share my good news. My mother's response was priceless. " I can hardly wait for you to bring her so I can meet her." I could tell by my mother's voice that she was happy for me. I tried calling Marcus, but he was still unavailable for calls. So I left a message on his cellphone of everything that had transpired since I moved to LA. Then I called Veronica and let her know Anna B. and I had gotten married. Veronica and Marcus were a lot alike. They both have always wanted nothing but the best for me. So, when Veronica told me she wished nothing but the best for me and Anna B., I knew she meant it.

Edward

"Two Weeks After Our Wedding"

I'd planned a 7-day cruise to Switzerland for our honeymoon. Anna B. and I boarded the ship on Sunday morning. For four consecutive days, we were livin' it up on the cruise ship. Once we got to Switzerland, I gave Anna B. one of my Visa Cards and told her she could shop as much as she liked. And, she and I would meet up again in two hours. I caught a trolley downtown to find Boris Borishnikoff, supposedly the finest jeweler in the world. The trolley driver, Juan, took me to Boris's Jewelry Store and asked if he should wait around. I told Juan I wasn't sure how long it would take me to find what I would be looking for. So, I wanted to pay my fare and have him return in an hour and a half to take me back to meet Anna B, but oddly, Juan didn't want to take his fare until after he picked me back up. As soon as he told me he would wait on his money, I thought to myself, 'This could never happen back in LA'. When I entered the Jewelry store, I saw what I wanted instantly. In a case all by themselves, there were two gorgeous bracelets. In my mind, these would make ideal gifts for two of the most important people in my life. I noticed a gentleman staring from behind a glass window as if he thought I was there to rob him. "How can I help you, sir?" the man asked. I am curious about these two bracelets, I said. "What about them, sir?" Well, If I were to purchase them both, could I ask you to engrave a few words across the center?" The gentleman looked at me with somewhat of a smirk on his face and said, "Sir, those two bracelets are 18 carat, White Diamonds. They cost 850,000.00 each. Perhaps, I'm almost certain you're looking for something a bit less expensive." My initial thought was that people will stereotype you no matter where you go. I wasn't offended by his comments at all. I've gone to places in LA and find their mindsets are the same way. As I was about to tell the gentleman how I really felt about his attitude, a taller gentleman walked up and said to me, "Excuse me, sir, my name is Boris; I happen to be the store's owner. I overheard how rude my employee, Nelson, was, and I would like to apologize for his behavior. As a matter of fact, I will excuse Nelson immediately, and I've got another employee, Izzy, who will be assisting you if you need anything at all," said Boris. Well, I thank you kindly, sir. In that case, I would like to purchase both of those bracelets, but I would need you to engrave a few words across the center of each of them. Would that be possible?" I asked. "What are the few words you'd like engraved," asked Boris. I wrote the words on a napkin, slid the owner my Black Card, and reminded him I was only in Switzerland for a few days and that I would need the jewelry done before the cruise ship pulled off on Monday. "That won't be a problem, sir. I will have Izzy start on these immediately. I shook Izzy's hand, tipped him two hundred, and told him I will be back soon.

Edward

Upon leaving the jewelry shop, I happened to stumble into a gift shop next door with a roll of Velcro hanging in the window. I immediately thought of my co-worker, Natalie, who seems to drop everything she touches. I started to smile to myself. "What seems to tickle you, sir," asked the clerk. "Oh, nothing too serious. The Velcro just reminded me of someone I know back in the States that can't seem to hold onto anything. I would like to purchase two rolls of it as a gift for that co-worker," I replied. Well, hopefully the recipient will understand the gesture is just a joke, and he or she won't try to tape everything in a bundle," joked the clerk. I Purchased the two rolls and paid the clerk to have them gift-wrapped. I'm sure Natalie will find the message in this rather cute.

I found what I was looking for much sooner than expected. So, I sat at an outside table that was under a well-manicured Oak tree next to the store to reflect on how much my entire life has changed since moving to LA. God has been truly good to me. I have accomplished so much in such a short time. I've invested in a few things of value. My biggest investment has been my Casino in Las Vegas. This investment has brought me profits I never could've imagined. I could retire today, spend a thousand dollars every single day, and still won't have financial concerns ever again in life. As a kid growing up in Atlanta, I've always loved a fancy Corvette. So, when I made my first million dollars, I went out and bought two of them. I gave both unique names. My Black corvette has red stripes along the sides. For that reason, I named it The Black Widow. It does everything on the dashboard and some. I named my other Corvette Floraine. It is red and has those stylish Halogen headlights, and the moment I saw it, it sent my 'RPMs through the roof. So, it was only fitting I named it after someone I knew back in the day that gave me a similar reaction. I love my cars equally as much as I love my mother, but when it comes to the one person I couldn't live without, that would be Anna B. I would give this woman the world on a silver platter if she asked for it. She is a handful to deal with at times, but I would rather have her to deal with than try to live my life without her.

Edward

'Last Day of The Cruise'

Our honeymoon was a blast! I called my trolley driver, Juan, to see if he would like to join Anna B. and me for lunch on our final day. He was such a patient driver, and after taking me back and forth for the past two days, I figured that was the least I could do. Juan declined the invite but told me he and his wife, Florina, might be visiting California in the near future and would gladly take me up on the offer when he gets there. On our final day in Switzerland, Anna B. and I visited some of the tallest mountains in the city, ate dinner at the world-renowned *La Maisonette,* visited one of the most interesting Museums in the world, and visited the most famous Chocolate Candy factories, the world has ever known. But, like most things, our time was coming to an end. It was time to pack our belongings and board the ship. I went by Boris's to pick up my jewelry. Just as I'd hoped, everything was perfect. I wasn't so surprised. Boris's reputation as being the best jeweler in the world is well deserved. I shook Boris's and Izzy's hands and told them how appreciative I was for their service. Anna B. and I boarded the cruise ship to head back to the States. Once the ship pulled away from the dock, I gave Anna B. one of the gifts I'd purchased from Boris's. Anna B. was curious to know what it was. "Just open it and see," I said. Anna B. slowly opened the gift as if she was nervous. When she saw what I'd purchased for her, her eyes lit up like a Christmas tree. "Hun, you mean the world to me. I don't ever want you to change," she whispered softly. "If a day should come and it seems I'd change somewhat, it must only mean I would love you more on that day than I do now. And I find that almost impossible to do," I replied. Anna B. got teary-eyed, winked at me, and said, "Hun, whenever you talk to me like that, my knees get weak. So, I'm gonna need you to pick me up, carry me to my bed, and put me to sleep. In that order, please." I winked back and said, "Say less."

Edward

'After The Cruise'

Everything between Anna B. and I had happened so fast that we didn't even discuss our living arrangements once we got married. I realized we could run into a dilemma because Anna B. didn't like my place, nor was I a fan of hers. Anna B. felt my apartment was more of a man cave than an apartment. And I wasn't so thrilled with her place because everything in her place was paisley; even her vacuum cleaner was completely floral. So, I remember Anna B. telling me a house on the hills was one of the things on her wishlist. I remember seeing a very nice mansion online when I first moved to LA that I loved, but it was way too large for one person at the time. But now that Anna B. and I have become one, that particular house would be ideal if it's still on the market. I went online and discovered the house was still on the market. I called up the realtor, Ms. A. Green, to let her know I was interested in looking at the house. Ms.Green and I had an outstanding relationship from back in the day. We met an hour later. I looked over the entire house. It was everything I anticipated. I was certain this would fit Anna' B's taste. I pulled out my checkbook, wrote a check for 50,000.00, handed it to Ms. Green, and asked her to write me up a contract, and I would come back by when she is done to sign it. "I don't usually do business like this, Mr. Keats, but I am making an exception this one time," said Ms. Green.

I knew Anna B. was still exhausted from our honeymoon, so I waited three days before I mentioned anything to her about our new place. On the fourth day, I called up my chauffeur, Virgil, and asked him to meet me at my apartment. He complied. I filled him in on how I wanted to surprise Anna B. with this house I'd just purchased. I filled Virgil in on all the minor details I'd like him to do. Then, Virgil and I drove over to Anna'B's place. I told Anna B. I had a surprise for her that required us to take a drive to where the surprise was. "Whatever you'd like, hun," said Anna.B. By the tone of her voice, I could tell I'd won her over somewhat. I had Virgil stop and purchase a bottle of Champagne on our way to Anna B's place. I mentioned to Anna B. that Virgil would be doing the driving to this surprise I had for her. "Fine by me," she said. As we slowly rode through Beverly Hills, I had every song Anna B. told me she liked downloaded onto a playlist. I could see the excitement in Anna'B's eyes as we rode through several affluent neighborhoods in LA. Anna B. was teary-eyed throughout. I wasn't sure if it was because of the many sips of champagne she had overindulged in, or the excitement of her favorite songs being played. But whatever the reason, it didn't matter. As long as she was happy. We pulled up to the driveway of our new mansion. "Whose house is this, and how long do we have it for?, asked Anna. B. I smiled, kissed her ever so gently, and said, "This is our new house, and it will be ours for as long as you and I are one," I replied. Anna B. gave me that familiar wink and said, I think you should send Virgil on his way, hun." I'd inform virgil to drive away the minute we enter the house," I said.

Edward

'The Next Morning'

The following morning, I was awakened by the smell of Bacon and a blender swirling at low speed. For a split second, I thought perhaps my mother may have snuck in and spent the night in one of the four bedrooms without my knowing. But much to my surprise, it was Anna B. cooking breakfast. I'd known Anna B. all this time, and she's never mentioned to me that she could cook. I walked up behind her, gently massaged her shoulders, and playfully asked, "What seems to be the occasion?" "Oh, don't get too relaxed because If I'd cooked for you sooner, I'm not so sure you would've married me," said Anna B. I wasn't sure if Anna B. was being sarcastic or, if she had acquired a dry sense of humor from the champagne the night before.

Edward

'After Breakfast'

When Anna B. got done eating breakfast, she asked, "What do you think of my cooking skills, babe?" Well, I didn't want to lie, nor did I want to hurt her feelings, so I quickly thought I would ask her something that would make her not be concerned with my answer. "Oh babe, did you really like the gift I bought you in Switzerland?" A smile came over Anna' B's face as bright as the gift I had designed for her. "Yes, of course I do. But then, all of your gifts are wonderful," said Anna B. My question seemed to have distracted Anna B. perfectly. She started crying. Then she ran upstairs to the Master Bedroom to wipe off the mascara that had dripped on the side of her face. When she ran upstairs, I immediately took our plates, scraped the rest of my meal in the disposal, and cleaned the kitchen thoroughly. I found out two important factors over breakfast. Anna B. is very sensitive and we won't be dining at home unless I am preparing our meal.

Virgil Bates

I was raised in Birmingham, Alabama. I had an awful childhood upbringing. I got involved with drugs and alcohol at an early age. My parents both died at an early age of natural causes. I never did understand what natural causes actually meant. I've always felt natural cause was a term used when coroners really didn't know the actual cause of death. My crazy side always felt this was a conspiracy theory, but I'm sure no one would listen to me even if I was correct. I have two sons, Terrance and Bobby, one twenty-two years old, the other twenty years of age. I haven't spoken to either of them in over ten years. I imagine they lost respect for me because of my irresponsible behavior. I can't really blame them. So, whenever people ask me, "Do you have any kids? I would always pretend as if I didn't hear the question. I feel it is better for people not to know I've got kids than to have them judge me for not being involved in my kid's lives. I've got issues I need to address. I pray one day I would be disciplined enough to avoid drugs and alcohol altogether. It seems I am fighting a war against myself every single day. However, I did play basketball in college. Or should I say I was on the team. Our coach would promise me he would let me in the game if I could stay clean for an entire week. Well, it is safe to say I wasn't good on holding up to my end of the bargain. I do wonder at times how things would've turn out if I was fully devoted to the sport of basketball. Unfortunately, I will never know. Years ago, I met a young lady by the name of Brenda Cee. She was intelligent, gorgeous and was as thick as Atlanta's 5.00pm traffic. She loved me and I knew it. But at that age, I wasn't sure how to reciprocate. As much as I adored her, sadly, I didn't understand love, and I allowed her to walk away and find someone else worthy of all the things she so deserved. My addiction, even way back then was something that would cost me dearly. I am somewhat glad things ended the way they did though. I would've end up being a disappointment to her, and that is something she didn't deserve. Quite honestly, I pray she is somewhere enjoying the type of life she'd promised me she and I would one day share.

Virgil

When I met Edward, it was as if I was given a second chance in life. I'd been in and out of rehab centers for alcohol and drugs for years. My former employer wasn't paying me top dollar, so when Edward offered me a job as his driver, plus a five thousand dollar sign-on deal, the decision to hop on board was an easy one. My former employer didn't like me very much, but they tolerated me because they knew they were paying me well below my value. So, I could hardly wait to inform them I wasn't interested in working for them anymore. Working for Edward was the right fit for me. He was a caring boss. He didn't allow my past mistakes to be a reason to look at me or treat me any differently. Sometimes, he would buy me nice gifts. It was his unique way of saying thank you. It seems Edward had a remarkable understanding of what I'd been through. I was in awe of him, mainly because I'm not sure I'd be as trusting or forgiving if the shoes were on the other foot. Edward was as good a boss as I'd ever come across. He wasn't demanding or overly concerned about what I did on my own time, as long as I was there when or if he needed me. He showed gratitude in everything someone did for him. He treated me more like a family than an employee. I often wondered how a man raised by a single mom, with no father figure to steer him in the right direction, got to be so blessed. I found myself envious at times. Not because of his success but more so because of his determination and work ethic. Yes, he has a smart, successful wife in Anna B., but I was more impressed of the rumor that had circled around that he made his own way on sheer determination, faith, and his belief in God. As a youngster, I heard people say these were the attributes that would take you farther than money, but to witness someone who was totally committed to those beliefs was something special.

Every now and then, Edward would ask me to drive him around affluent neighborhoods like Brentwood, Beverly Hills, or the Bel Air areas. I always thought he had ideas for opening a business of some sort, but I didn't want to ask. And besides, he was secretive in his own way. He kept his business to himself but always left his heart open. He would always say, "If you ever need anything at all, don't hesitate to ask." Edward never spoke about business or money in my presence. He was an extremely sharp individual when it comes to business. With businesses abroad, working at a law firm, and being married, I wondered how he balanced everything. I imagine with no kids; things were somewhat manageable. Anna B. and Edward seem like the perfect power couple. I've never heard of one single disagreement between the two. I often look at my life and wonder why I wasn't farther ahead in life as they were. But then those thoughts would take me back to those rehab centers as a reminder and the answer to my own question.

Virgil

I truly believe if I wasn't working for Edward, I would be totally strung out on drugs and alcohol. Working for Edward inspired me to be a better person. I look at where he came from, his determination, how focused he was coming from a small town in Atlanta, and where he is today, and I realize that anything is possible. I noticed also that he wasn't overly concerned about where Anna B. goes or how long she stays out. I always thought if I were in his position, I might think differently. Unique, might be the perfect word to describe their relationship. Sometimes, Anna B. would be gone for weeks at a time, and they both seemed so content. I've gotten so used to Anna B. saying to me, "Virgil, I need you to pick me up in the morning. I've got to catch my 8:00 am flight." It seems as if all of her flights were at the exact time each month. It was like they had another life outside of their marriage.

I found myself looking in the mirror many nights. My kids are grown, and I've never been married, but I've got nothing to show for it but a long history of failed relationships with women. Maybe I need to change my perspective, I thought. I keep telling myself I should be more like Edward. Maybe when it comes to women, I should be more trusting, or perhaps, believe in them more. But when I turn away from the mirror, I realize that isn't me. It takes a special kind to be Edward. And I am not that person. As much as I admired Edward, I'd rather have his work ethic and determination in business than his sense of trust. In my opinion, Anna B. was smart, caring, and successful, but there was something about her that told me Edward was more in love with her than she was with him. As I would drive her to the airport to catch her early morning flights, she would say flirtatious one-liners that raised my eyebrow. I wasn't sure if she was testing me or if it was her strange sense of humor. I would always smile as if it was a joke, just so nothing would be taken out of context. I live a boring life. I live in solitude pretty much. I don't have a lot of friends. I consider Veronica to be the only friend I have. See, I've grown to not trust anyone. I've been stabbed in the back so many times, the scars sit as a reminder the few of times I did trust. My family and I are distant. I looked out for most of them before I got on drugs, but not one of them came to see me while in rehab. The second time I went to rehab, I wasn't so surprised that no one came to see me. I'd accepted the fact that my problems are no one else's. There's no one else to blame. So when I got out, I changed my telephone number and gave up everyone who had given up on me.

Chapter Four
Marcus Irvin Anderson

As a kid, I remember watching my mother, *"Mama Johnson,"* stand in cold, rainy Atlanta weather to catch the city bus to work. She would do this Monday through Friday every week for many years. She hired a babysitter to watch after me while she worked. Some days, I could sense she was getting tired. Though I was young, I could hardly wait for the day when I would be old enough to work and help her with the expenses around the house. Sometimes, when she got in from work, I'd be asleep in my bedroom. I would be awakened the next morning by the chirping of birds from the tree limb that overlapped my window sill or the smell of fresh bacon frying as she prepared breakfast. Every morning before work, she would enter my room, remind me to do my chores around the house, then kiss me goodbye. She would then sit around in the living room until the babysitter, Christie, arrived. Sometimes, I would sit in the living room with her until it was time for her to leave. Saturday was her rest day, and Sunday was our day, when we'd attend church, and afterward we would have dinner, then discuss everything from my father, who died in a car accident a few years ago, to what our future plans consist of. In our neighborhood of Decatur, Georgia, we had five families that got along well. However, my mother didn't interact much with any of them. Though she never deterred me from hanging out with the other kids, she wasn't one to mingle. She was always private. I often thought it was her heavy workload that kept her to herself until one Sunday afternoon after church, I finally opened up and asked her what she thought of the neighborhood and why she doesn't mingle with the other neighbors. Shockingly, she looked at me and said, "Finish eating your dessert, and I will share my thoughts after you're done." As good as my mom's Apple Pie was, I could hardly wait to hear what she had to say. I took two bites of my pie, pushed it to the side, grabbed the remote to the television, pressed the mute button so there wouldn't be any distractions, and let her have her say. My mother said, *"Son, I've been hurt many times in my life. I don't blame anyone for that. My pain and regret come from relying on others to assist me. Since the day your father and I got married, he provided for you and me both. However, the pain I experience daily of not having him around can't be described in words alone. See, after his death, there were so-called friends who said I could reach out to them if I ever needed anything. To this day, not a single one has answered my calls or returned any of my emails when I needed them the most. As painful as that may sound, it was more eye-opening than anything. I've learned that people may have good intentions, but that doesn't mean they are always willing. So, I've learned to trust only in God. I truly believe I was allowed to go through those adverse experiences so I would be able to alarm you about how cold this world could be. I would like for you to learn from my experiences so you won't end up relying on anyone other than God."*

It was the most eye-opening conversation my mother and I had ever had. And, it was a conversation I would always remember!

Marcus

'Reflecting Back'

As I look at life in retrospect, I remember when I first got interested in music. I recall one day, while my mom was at work, I decided to listen to an old Blues CD by BB King that had been sitting on my mother's dresser for some time. I was inspired by the artist, his music, and the passion in which he played. My mom told me how much my dad had always loved Jazz music. So, I was certain this was one of his CD's my mom decided to keep as sentimental value in his honor. Listening to this CD motivated me. I took all the money I'd saved up from the allowances my mom had been giving me over the years, bought a quality guitar, and worked on my craft every single day. All the while, my only two friends, Veronica and Edward, had been preoccupied doing their own thing. Veronica had started dating her high school sweetheart back in the day, and Edward was attending school at Emory University. Edward was considered the brainy one of our small circle. He loved school and Poetry. I was good at a lot of different things, but I decided I wanted to make my career in music. I got really good at playing the guitar. Over time, I would emulate my favorite artist, Prince. One afternoon, when Edward came over to visit during spring break, he heard me playing. He asked, "When did you learn to play?" While you were in school at Emory, I said. Edward sat in disbelief as I picked BB King's, 'Lucille,' without missing a beat. "You need to start recording your material, Marcus; you never know when a band might need a great guitarist. You could then perform onstage," said Edward. "I've already spoken to Jay Cruz, leader of "The

All-Nighters," the popular band from Union City, and he'd asked me to come down to their studio so he could take a listen at what I could do," I replied. "Awesome. Keep me informed on how things turn out. I'm sure you're going to do well, though," said Edward.

Edward had to leave to check on his mother, LaDonna, whom I haven't seen in almost a year. So we shook hands like old times, and off to his mom, he went. "Please tell your mother I said hello," I yelled as Edward was backing out of my driveway. "I definitely will," said Edward.

I had my trial with the 'All-Nighters' two weeks later. The band loved how well I performed. I was hired instantly. We had gigs lined up for two consecutive months. We played at gigs from 9.00 PM to 3.00 AM. Money was decent, but it wasn't my idea of being successful.

Marcus

Our band had become so popular that every gig was a definite sellout. Of course, the club owners were happy, and even the other members of the band seemed content, but I had a bigger dream. I wanted more. My plan was to address Steve, our manager, before our next gig and let him know I wasn't interested in playing with the band after Friday. I thought it would give him ample time to find a replacement for me. But, on Wednesday, two days before our next gig, Steve called and asked if I could meet with him in his office at 1.00 pm to discuss a business matter over lunch. I agreed. I thought it might be an ideal time to let Steve know how I felt. When I arrived at Steve's office, his secretary, Brianna, whom I'd just met just two weeks ago, welcomed me with an unusual greeting. She smiled and said, "Hi Kos, Steve will be right with you." It's not unusual for someone you've met only once to forget your name, I thought. Steve walked in two minutes later, shook my hand, and asked me to have a seat. He wasn't one to waste time. He's always said, "Time is Money." He read from a typed letter that Brianna apparently had just dropped on his desk while greeting me. "With the recent exposure and demand the band has been getting, I will be increasing the portions of the proceeds for each band member by seventy-five dollars per member. Plus, Marcus, because you've been such an attraction with your guitar playing, you would get an extra two hundred dollars." Quite nice of you, Steve, I said rather nonchalantly. I assume the reason none of the others are here is because I got a much larger raise than they did?" I asked. "That would be correct," said Steve. He then pointed at a banner on the wall behind him, which read, "You the Man, KOS." Somewhat confused, I asked, "Who is KOS?" Steve smiled and said, KOS is a nickname you've earned. It stands for "King of the Strings" because of your unique ability to play the hell out that guitar." Tickled and flattered at the same damn time, I gave Steve a hug and thanked him for everything. As hard as this was, I had to tell Steve that Friday night would be my last night playing with the band. I also mentioned to him that I had another dream I wanted to pursue. The Look on Steve's face appeared as if he'd just lost a best friend. "Are you sure I can't change your mind, brother, asked Steve. "My mind is made up. However, I would appreciate it if you would split the increase in pay among the other members equally, I replied. "I can do that, and I'm willing to pay you more if it would convince you to change your mind," said Steve. Thanks, but that won't be necessary. However, there is one thing I'd like to ask of you," I said. "What's that? Steve asked excitedly. "Can I keep that nickname?" "Of course, you can, KOS," Steve said. We shook hands, and I told him I would see him on Friday.

Marcus

Friday seemed to have come so quickly. We jammed to a sellout crowd of over two hundred people for five straight hours. I did my usual fifteen-minute solo act, which had become a main feature at local clubs. It was my final night with the band. I could tell the other band members were fully aware of my leaving because of the passion in which they were playing. Tonight, unlike other nights, they seem to have been playing with much more passion than usual. Plus, I am certain Steve might've informed the rest of the band of the increase in pay and that tonight was my final night with them. We 'jammed' all night long, it seemed. Every CEO, business owner, and drug dealer I'd ever known was in attendance. When the show was over, I decided to hang out for a while. I got to mingle with some of the most powerful people in Atlanta. All the while, I was picking their brains, earning their trust, but more importantly, studying how and with whom the drug dealers operated. After each conversation, I paid close attention to everyone in the room. I listened carefully while the 'Big-wigs' boasted about the many things they owned and how they managed to launder their 'dirty money' in legit businesses. I noticed how proudly they spoke about the many areas in the city that they claimed as 'Their turfs'. I made a mental note of everything I heard.

Marcus

I took advantage of the fact that most of the CEOs and Drug Dealers knew of me. I was given a business card from each of them on my final night with the band. I remembered what Steve always said; 'Time is money.' So, after the show, I decided to immediately contact "Iron Head," supposedly the most powerful drug dealer in the Atlanta area. I took the money I'd saved up from the many gigs I'd performed at. I bought a substantial amount of 'Good-Good ' and hired a staff of seven people I grew up with. I made sure to hire only people I've known previously in some capacity. Vivian Feliz was my first hire. She was always good with numbers in high school, so I knew she was capable of handling large sums of money. I made her my accountant. Nathaniel Munoz and Joe 'Money' Fritz were former high school football players. They stood 6'6 and 6'8, respectively. I hired them as my bodyguards. I then hired "Bone-Head" Braxton and "One-Eye" Broadhurst as my salesmen. I remember as kids, those two could sell snow to an Eskimo. And lastly, I hired Rose Taylor and Chaz Perez as my 'Spies'. They seemed headstrong and courageous, even as kids. So, I knew they would fit in well with my plan. I trained my staff thoroughly about everything from being punctual to being ready to drop everything and be ready to flee at any given moment. To get my staff accustomed to money, I took them on trips around the world, bought them extravagant gifts, and treated them to some of the finest restaurants in North America. During our first week in operation, we made over 100,000.00. The following week, we tripled that amount. Each week, we progressed to new heights. I got so big I bought a turf of my own next to " ELEGANTE PALISUADES', one of the nicest areas of Atlanta. I registered my mother into the exact retirement facility Edward had his mother stay in. Everything was falling into place, just as Edward and I had talked about when we were teens. I loved the facility's logo on the door, "*A Suite For The Sweetest.* I moved my mother two doors down from Edward's mother, LaDonna, just so she would have someone she could chat with on a daily basis. I could've easily had my mother stay in one of the five houses I'd purchased throughout Atlanta, but I didn't want her to feel like she was alone. I taught my staff to always be cautious about their surroundings at all times and sleep lightly. My motto for my staff was, "If a roach happens to crawl in your bathroom while you're lying in your bedroom, you should be able to hear it."

Marcus

(Six months later)

The last few months, I'd been so busy executing my plan I didn't have time to return anyone's phone calls. I made a promise almost a year ago to my mom and Edward, who had wisely moved out to Los Angeles, California, that everything would be okay, hopefully within a year. I'd been so busy designing my plan that I didn't realize I'd missed about 30 phone calls, 10 of which were from Edward. Surprisingly, one of Edward's messages was that he was so blessed to have gotten a job at a world-renowned Law Firm and doing well. However, the most shocking news of all was that Edward said that he had met an interesting lady that he wanted to get married to. He also mentioned that he would like me to attend and be his 'Best Man' at their wedding. Unfortunately, I am just now noticing these messages. I tried calling Edward immediately, but I got no response. So, I ended up leaving a message on his voicemail explaining my reason for being MIA for the past eight to nine months. I also explained to him I wouldn't have missed his wedding day for nothing in the world if I hadn't been so busy. Edward has always been a stand-up and understanding friend. He knew if I was able to be there, I would.

Marcus

'Three Months Later'

I've always been loyal to my staff. I treated them as if they were family. However I started to notice a sharp decrease in revenue being deposited into my accounts. I started paying closer attention to my staff. I paid each of them well over six figures. When I was outlining my plan for my operation, one of the most valuable investments I purchased was a desk made of Sandalwood from overseas. I had a hidden camera installed with audio that came with a remote control. I stored the desk in one of my warehouses on Buford Highway. Once I purchased the building for my operation, I had the movers install my desk in my place of operation immediately. I prayed I would never have to keep an eye out for anyone stealing, so I locked the remote control in my safe at home. But it seems I've got a problem I need to address. I called a meeting to see if anyone had a financial issue I could help with. I didn't mention anything about my missing funds. I thought that my asking if anyone needed my assistance would open up room for an honest discussion. But not one of my staff members came forward. So, I then had to have a one-on-one meeting with my accountant, Vivian. I gave her two weeks to replace the funds, and no questions would be asked. Meanwhile, I went home and unlocked my safe to retrieve the remote control for the desk. I was a bit shaken about this entire theft. As crazy as this sounds, I hoped this was all a miscalculation on Vivian's part.

Marcus

The idea that someone in my staff would steal from me never crossed my mind. However, I started going over Vivian's paperwork from the beginning of the second week of operation. So, for two consecutive days, I stayed away from my staff. I replayed the audio recorder's messages and watched videos from the time we started my operation to the current. I listened to every single conversation my employees had with one another carefully. I wanted to see if any of the messages or conversations could somehow be a link to my missing funds. Much to my dismay, I learned that my entire staff had played a part. They had all been connected to the theft in some way or another. I did the only thing I could think of at the time. I called my friend Edward in California. I mentioned to him how I had been deceived and was not sure what I was going to do about it. I know I couldn't just fire everyone at once. Edward told me to act as if nothing was wrong, and he would come up with a plan to nab the culprits. Meanwhile, it became tough to face my own staff with the same face.

Marcus

So, while waiting to see what plan Edward could come up with, I began taking 'Hits' from the very product I supplied. It was the only way I could face my staff without wringing their necks off. I became dependent on the substance. It was the only thing I could use to disguise the anger I had built up. My entire empire started to fall apart right before my eyes. I stopped caring about everything. The only thing that mattered to me anymore was my mother. I made sure I paid her rent six months in advance. Two weeks went right by, and my funds had not been replaced. I got so 'zooted up' one Friday afternoon I went into the office and fired every one of my staff members. Then, I sat at my desk and snorted until I couldn't snort anymore. I got so high I still don't remember how I ended up on the side of the road in the middle of the night in Sandy Springs, Georgia. I was told I was found on a side street off Roswell Road by an undercover Police officer. To this day, I don't know if I was kidnapped, robbed, then thrown on the side of the street, or if I walked that far on my own. I have no recollection of anything of that Friday except the fact that I fired my entire staff. As a matter of fact, I don't remember much of anything after that night. I woke up the following day at Piedmont Hospital with tubes of liquid hanging over my head. For a split second, I thought I'd died and went to Heaven. Everyone around me was dressed in white. I could vaguely see someone wearing an Atlanta Falcons football cap speaking with another person dressed in a white coat. This was like a dream or a movie. And I was so intrigued by how this entire episode would end I hurriedly closed my eyes to try and track the outcome of this bizarre dream.

Marcus

'At Rehab Center in LA'

I woke up to the sounds of sirens and sensors all around me. I started to see people I'd never seen before. I could hardly wait to ask the gorgeous young nurse passing by where I was. The nurse said, "You are here at Kaiser/Dior's Rehab center in Los Angeles, California. A gentleman by the name of Edward Keats registered you in. He has also informed us to have you call him the minute you wake up. He told us you should have his number, but just in case your memory is clouded from the drugs that were throughout your system, he left it on a piece of paper, which is attached to your belongings in your room. Lastly, Mr. Keats has arranged for his Limo driver, Virgil Bates, to pick you up as soon as you wake up. You will be staying with him at his mansion." How long was I here? I asked. "Sir, you were here for exactly twenty-eight days. And, your entire bill was paid for by Mr.Keats as well.

I immediately thought I should call my mother to inform her of my whereabouts the past month. I'm sure she's worried out of her mind right now. I called my mom, but I couldn't seem to reach her. I called back ten minutes later, and still no answer. When I tried calling a third time, I was interrupted by a tall gentleman who had walked up to me, introduced himself as Virgil Bates, Edward's limo driver, and informed me he was assigned to take me wherever I needed to go from this day moving forward. He then took my belongings and asked me to follow him.

Marcus

I immediately detected a negative vibe about Edward's limo driver, Virgil. He seemed jittery. As a drug dealer, I could tell a 'user' if he was a thousand miles away and covered in snow. While on our way to Edward's place, Virgil told me how fortunate he was to still be alive. He said he had no family members he can call on for anything. He went on further to tell me he'd been battling a drug addiction for many years. I actually found him to be quite talkative, to say the least. "So, how long have you and Edward been friends, Marcus?" Forever, brother. What made you ask, I replied. "Well, he boasts about you often," said Virgil. "Is that right? I asked. Oh yes, brother. He talks about how well you can play a guitar. And, in case you didn't know, Edward thinks the world of you, brother," said Virgil. Of course, I know this. He and I are ' blood Boys. We would die for each other," I said. I was certain there must be something about Virgil that Edward sees in him to keep him around. Edward has always believed in giving someone a fair opportunity. So, I just let Virgil talk until we reached our destination. When we finally arrived at Edward's place, I noticed Virgil seemed to have the urge to get a 'hit'. He kept scratching his arms. Then he would bite on his bottom lip. I knew what his problem was, but it wasn't my concern. I decided to pretend as if I didn't notice anything wrong. Virgil parked the limo. He then helped me gather my possessions, brought them to Edward's door, and told me he would be available whenever I called. I thanked him and wished him a safe trip home. I then rang Edward's doorbell. I could hear Edward's footsteps from the outside, walking towards the door. From the sound of his footsteps, it seems he has gained quite a few pounds since

I last saw him. (We greet each other). "My brother, what's been going on, Edward?"

Marcus

(Meeting Edward for the first time in LA)

Edward and I talked for hours. He smiled broadly when I asked him about his job at the firm. "The best job I've ever had," said Edward. Edward's demeanor changed when I asked him about his co-workers at the firm. He spoke extensively about his co-workers. He first started out talking about Tammy Richardson. "She is by far the sweetest woman I've ever met and a damn great secretary." "I've got a Natalie Owens that works right next to me. Brilliant worker, but drops everything she touches. She seems to have grease on her fingers. She cannot hold onto anything. She goes to great measures in anything she believes in, though. And she speaks her mind. Edward adds," I've got a Rosalind Butler at the firm that is a handful in her own right. She seems to think the world owes her something. She complains every single day, to the point where I've gotten so accustomed to her, I just excuse myself to the restroom. By the time I return, she has no one else to complain to, so then she goes about her work in a normal fashion," said Edward. Of all my co-workers, our child-hood friend, Veronica, and Tammy seems to be the only ones that are problem-free." Well, tell me, Edward, how is it working alongside your wife, Anna B, in the same department? I asked. "Well, Anna B. is hardly ever there. She gets sent to Dubai monthly, which is actually a good thing. She's the executive that handles business affairs with other countries. She gets paid the big bucks, Marcus. She loves money like you wouldn't believe." Let's just hope she doesn't love money more than she does you, Edward," I said. Edward's reply was, "Well, I'll just hope there won't come a time where she'd have to decide between money or me. I'm not sure I'd stand a chance," laughs Edward. I'm not sure if Edward was joking or if he'd adopted a dry sense of humor since moving to LA. So I decided to change the subject. "So, it seems LA has been good for you, brother," I said. A broad smile came upon Edward's face. "It certainly has been. I've been blessed, for sure. "Oh 'snaps, I almost forgot. Marcus, I've got a business meeting with a gentleman in less than an hour. And Anna B. is due back from Dubai at 10.00 a.m. tomorrow. So I've got to get things moving along. I will cook dinner for us when I get back. But before I head out, I would like you to have this key to my Red Classic Corvette stored in the garage out back. Also, here's a box with 50 000.00 cash. If you decide you'd like to start your life over again here in LA, it would be a start. And lastly, I bought this gift for you while Anna B. and I were on vacation in Switzerland. There are only two of these in the world. I had them custom-made. I'd like you to have the other one," said Edward.

Marcus

"Man, I'm not sure how to begin to thank you," Edward. "You don't have to, Marcus. I am certain you would've done the same for me, brother," replied Edward. Edward checked his watch again as if he'd over-extended his time. "I've gotta run, Marcus. Whatever you decide, it would be all good." Edward grabbed his sports coat, gave me a fist bump and a hug, reminded me he would cook dinner for us when he returns, and heads out the door. I'd already decided half-heartedly that I would be going back to Atlanta tomorrow. I like standing on my own two feet. I will definitely let Edward know this over dinner later. But before I head back to Atlanta, I've got to check out the West Coast's nightlife. So, I shaved, took a shower, and got dressed. I called Virgil to see if he could take me to a nice Jazz Bar. "I'd be there in twenty minutes," replied Virgil. I noticed Virgil was always ready to go. Great quality, I thought. While I waited for Virgil, I decided to open the boxed gift Edward had just given me. I slowly unwrapped the gift. It was so neatly wrapped, I didn't want to ruin the paper. I carefully opened the case, and much to my surprise, it was the most beautiful gift I've ever come across. It was an 18 carat White Diamond bracelet. Across the center, Edward had "One Hand Washes the Other" engraved in small diamonds. My first thought was I should wear it to the Jazz Bar tonight. But then, I didn't want to be too flamboyant. So I decided to put it back in the case and just keep it as a piece I would always treasure.

Marcus

'Waiting For Virgil'

While waiting for Virgil, I got on the phone and booked my flight for 8.00 a.m. Saturday morning. The receptionist kept putting me on hold. While waiting for her to get my Departure Time together, I looked around and noticed Edward's front room seemed rather empty. Oddly, the walls were bare. There's not one picture of any kind anywhere. I recall Edward telling me he'd finally finished all of his Poetry he'd started on back in Atlanta, but he must have them hidden, or he must've sold them all. The receptionist finally got my flight set for 8.00 a.m., and Virgil pulled in at the same time. "Yes, I yelled out as Virgil parked his limo. I've got to ask Edward later why he doesn't have any pictures in this huge mansion over dinner. I opened the door to let Virgil in. "What type of club are you interested in, brother," asked Virgil. Take me to the nicest Jazz club you know of, I said.

Marcus

We drove about fifteen minutes on the Boulevard. Virgil exited off the Boulevard, where a sign read, 'Welcome To The Lion's Den.' "This is the nicest club in LA," said Virgil. What makes this one nicer than the others, I asked. "Everyone here has money," said Virgil. "What time would you like me to pick you up, Marcus?" asked Virgil. About two hours from now. I want a chance to chat with Edward over dinner before I head back to the 'ATL' tomorrow. "I will see you in a couple of hours then," said Virgil. I went inside this club. The music was definitely different. It seemed like a mix of Pop, R&B, and contemporary, all in one. I sat at the bar. The red-haired bartender, with the name 'Jen', on her nametag, asked, "Would you like one 'up top or 'down low?" I had no clue what she was asking. So, I decided to take the safe route. I said, 'Jen, I would like an 'Arnold Palmer' please. She looked at me as if I was a resident of Pluto. 'Are you sure that's all you can handle, rich guy?" In my mind, I felt she was being sarcastic. But I was not about to let her ruin my night. "Yes, Jen. That is all I can handle for now," I said. I believed she thought I was being cheap, but I really didn't know what the hell 'Up Top or 'Down Low' actually meant. I also remembered what my mother told me as a kid. She said, "Son, you never want to create a problem with anyone that cooks your meal or stirs your drink." So, I tried to be as cooperative as possible.

Marcus

'Meeting Betty'

As I sat enjoying the vibes and listening to Jen making petty remarks because of my choice of beverage, I noticed, at the far end of the bar, someone looking directly at me as if they knew me. I did a double-take and realized my eyes were not fooling me. There was this drop-dead, gorgeous woman staring at me. The way she was staring, I thought I should ask her if we'd met somewhere before. But before I could move towards her, she was already headed my way. She leaned over, then softly whispered, "Hello, my name is Betty. And I'm going to assume you're from the South?" she asked." Well, yes, I am. I'm from Atlanta, Georgia, I replied. "So, does this Southern man have a name? Oh wait, before you answer, I remember you southern boys prefer to use initials instead of your government names. So what's yours? she asked. My first thought was that she's going to think I'm being a smartass when I tell her my initials are MIA. So, I pondered over what I should say to this woman so she wouldn't think I was being a smartass with my response. As I was about to make up a fictitious name to use, Betty said "Wait, you're taking too long with your reply. I wouldn't want you to give me a name you wouldn't remember a week from now. So, tonight, I'm calling you Mike. I don't even need to know your real name. Whatever your real name is doesn't even matter," said Betty. Okay, then Mike, I am," I replied. My thought was, I am only here for one night, so I am okay being a 'Mike' for a few more hours.

Marcus

'An Hour Later'

While Betty and I sat sharing a conversation about how fortunate she was to still be alive after nearly escaping the wildfire that had burnt itself out the night before, Jen yelled across the bar, "Would you care for another powerful *Arnold Palmer*, sir?" Her sarcasm was starting to irritate me. I know I was never going to see her again, so I thought I would 'throw a few 'stones' of my own. "I would like another, Jen. And while you're at it, Would you put less alcohol in it? I could hardly taste the Vitamin C in the last one." Jen smiled, but I was certain her comeback would be much sharper the next time around. Betty and I talked for another hour or so. Our conversation was more about the 1996 bombing in Atlanta's Centennial Park. Betty told me she'd just left that park twenty minutes before the explosion. Her story was so intriguing I forgot to ask her if she lived there at some point. Suddenly, it was as if Betty got tired of the small talk. She leaned over and said, "Listen, Mike, you and I have been chatting about bullshit for far too long. It's time we 'cut through the chase'. I find you quite attractive. I've got a Penthouse no one knows about. It's not far from here. I don't usually do this, but tonight, I am willing to do something out of the ordinary. Why don't you and I leave this wild music and go to my place and listen to something more Jazzy?"

Marcus

Betty paid my tab of 25.00, which I thought was outrageously expensive for a non-alcoholic beverage. She then called valet to bring her car around the front. The valet pulls up in this Emerald Green, Mabach 57. I wasn't so surprised, though. Betty seemed to have had her 'Ducks in A Row'. "Hop in, let's go, Mike, she yelled. " I opened the passenger's door, and the first thing I noticed was a half-karat diamond embedded in the center of the steering wheel. "Not a bad 'piece, Betty," I said. "Well, thank you, Mike. You seem to have good taste yourself." How can you tell?, I asked, "Well, you chose me, didn't you?" We both laughed. I started to pay close attention to any landmark just so I'd know how to find my way back if this gorgeous woman turns into a wild woman, and I've got to scramble. We rode about seven miles. Betty makes a right turn off the interstate onto an unlit roadway. "Why is this street so dark? I asked. "Unlike you guys back in the South, you preserve the life of Sea Turtles by keeping it dark, whereas I simply like to think I glow better in the dark," said Betty. She does have a way with words, I thought. We get to a portion of the drive where the driveway is neatly layered with bricks. Then, about twenty-five feet further, there's a gate that sits about fifty yards from the penthouse. This lady definitely loves her space, I thought to myself. Betty grabs a remote from her glovebox and presses a button on the remote that is supposed to open the gate, but nothing happened."Damn, no good maintenance men I've got are useless. They'd supposed to have my gate repaired by the time I return home, but obviously, they didn't listen. Men never do what they are asked to," yells Betty. "Mike, will you please open your door and wave your hand four times in front of the sensor, asked Betty. I got out of the passenger's seat and waved my hands four times in front of the sensor, as Betty had informed me. Sure enough, the gate opens slowly. I got back in the passenger's seat, and we slowly cruised up to her Penthouse.

Marcus

'At Betty's'

Betty parked the car in the driveway and rushed to open the door. "Follow me, Mike, whispered Betty. I realized as Betty went up the steps to her Penthouse she was equally as fine as a grain of salt. But I didn't want to overreact or say anything that might ruin the moment. So, I remained cool so Betty wouldn't think I was desperate or 'thirsty' in any way. Betty opened the door, and we walked along the hallway that connects to her living room area. Betty says, "Mike, make yourself at home. I'm going to the bathroom to take a hot shower. I want to freshen up. Feel free to do whatever you like." When Betty went to shower. I decided to go back to the hallway, where I'd seen two poems hanging on the wall that piqued my curiosity. One of the poems was titled *Incognito,* which I thought was brilliantly written, and the other one was simply titled *Love.* I could hardly wait for Betty to exit the shower for a couple of reasons. My main reason was I would like to ask her who the poems were written by. The poems told me the author had a unique way of expressing his or her feelings. Even though the words seemed as if I'd heard them somewhere before, I found them to be eloquently written from the heart.

Marcus

I hear the water slow to a drip from the shower. I took a seat on a cozy, Crocodile Leather love seat. Betty yells from the bathroom, "Mike, are you okay, dear?" Yes, I'm good, I replied. Betty walks from the shower, partly- covered in a towel. Beads of water were glistening from her caramel skin. She was definitely what I consider *Eye-Candy*. Her skin was glowing like an evening sunset over the Pacific Ocean; Her eyes were as captivating as the water in the Carribeans; She sprayed a fragrance over her body that moved me like a Tornado ripping through a Paper Mill;. I was curious as to what the name of the perfume was called. So I asked Betty, "Who was the fragrance made by?" Betty says, "So, you would like to purchase another bottle of it for me?" It might be something I would consider, I said. "Well, you do seem like a class act," said Betty. "The perfume is called *Clive Christian, No.1*. It cost 825.00 a bottle." I will keep that in mind, I said. "Mike, are we going to talk about perfume all night, or we're going to relax and get comfy? You seem nervous. I promise I won't bite," said Betty. I took my shirt off and walked over to Betty's night table to lay my shirt over the edge. I thought for a split second my eyes may have been playing tricks on me. On that small table, Betty had precious jewelry spread out. Betty grabbed a remote control and started playing some really soothing Jazz tunes from her playlist. She then grabbed a bottle of wine from her wine chest. She asked if I would like to join her for a drink. I reminded her that I was not a drinker. "I remember. I was testing to see if you would lie to me," replied Betty. There was a slight breeze coming in from an opened window from her kitchen area. To be quite honest, I was somewhat nervous. My adrenaline started to rush through my veins. For some odd reason, I immediately thought for a split second I was losing my mind. I couldn't believe what I'd just seen on the table next to my shirt. So, I needed to get a closer look."Are you okay, Mike?" Betty asked. I could hardly get a word out of my own mouth. I looked upward as if something had flown in my eye. Then, slowly downward so I could get a good look at what had caught my attention in the first place. Much to my surprise, I saw an exact bracelet like the one Edward had given me a few hours earlier. '*One Hand Washes the Other*' embedded in diamonds across the center. I knew right away this was one of Edward's side chicks he never told me about. "What seems to be your problem, Mike?" Betty asked. I didn't know what to say. I grabbed my shirt off her dresser and said, " I seemed to have come down with a stomach virus all of a sudden. Would it be a problem if I asked you to drop me off back at the bar, Betty? "Oh, hell no. You must got confused me with Southern women. I don't handle rejection well. Are you out of your mind right now, Mike?" I couldn't say a word. " Hold up. No, I'm going to pretend you didn't just reject me. Then again, on second thought, you probably couldn't handle a woman like me anyhow." I could tell Betty was furious, but I didn't want to get involved romantically with anyone who was involved with my best friend, Edward, in some way, shape, or form.

Marcus

'Drive Back to the Bar'

Betty stops talking altogether. She goes to her bathroom, gets dressed, and asks, "Are you ready to go?" Yes, of course, I replied. For a split second, I thought she was going to tell me to find my own way back to the bar. But surprisingly, she remained classy throughout. I wanted to ask Betty how well she knows my best friend, Edward. But the way she sped off from her driveway, I knew she was not in the mood to answer anything I had to ask. So, I sat in the passenger's seat and chilled. We got a few miles down the roadway; Betty finally slowed her car down and said, "Listen, Mike, or whatever your name is, after I let you out, I'm not sure we will ever meet again. You're headed back to Atlanta tomorrow and don't have an idea what you're going to do there." Betty adds, "I've got this business proposition for you that I'd like you to consider." Let me hear it then, I replied. "My husband is filthy rich. He pays me less attention than you just did. I am willing to offer you two hundred fifty thousand dollars to kill him. You would easily get away with it. You'd be back in Atlanta before anyone even realizes something is wrong. So, are you interested?" If we're talking cash, I might. But that would be something I would have to think over," I said. "Good, think it over, and I will give you a call later." I didn't put a lot of emphasis on what Betty had said. I just wanted her to believe I would at least entertain the thought. I could hardly wait to see Edward to ask him if he knew how dangerous this side chick of his truly is. And, judging from the bracelet she has, it is apparent they had or still have a deep relationship of some sort.

Marcus

'Drive Back at The Bar'

Betty dropped me off back at 'The Lion's Den' Bar. I then called Virgil and asked if he could pick me up. "Certainly. I will be there in twenty minutes," replied Virgil. As usual, twenty minutes later, Virgil was pulling up to the Bar. "I hope you had a good time, Marcus, said Virgil." I had an interesting evening, brother. I knew how much of a talker Virgil was, so before he started inquiring about details of my Evening, I told him I didn't care to discuss how my night had ended. I did remind Virgil I've got to be at the airport to catch my flight back to Atlanta at 8.00.AM. "I didn't forget, brother," said Virgil. Have you heard anything from Edward, Virgil?" "No, I haven't. But Edward is known to be gone for days at a time without telling anyone," said Virgil. His comment did give me a sense of easement. Although I still wished I could verbally thank him for everything he's done for me, But I imagine I would just have to leave a note for him instead. We pull up to Edward's Mansion. I got out of the car, thanked Virgil, and told him I would see him in a few hours. I went inside and sat on Edward's loveseat so that if Edward were to walk in, I wouldn't miss him. I must've fallen asleep immediately. Seemed as if I kept hearing this ringing in my ear. It felt like my eyes had been closed for only a minute or two. It shouldn't be my alarm clock to get up already. I looked at my watch, then back at my cell phone. I realized it was my phone ringing, and I was certain it must be Edward finally calling to check on me. I grabbed the phone and started a conversation immediately. "Hey brother, I've been worried sick about you. Where have you been?" I asked. The voice on the other end responded, "Obviously, this isn't who you'd expected. This is Betty. Did you think about the business proposition I offered you?" asked Betty. No, I haven't. I fell asleep, I replied. Betty went on a rant. "I was hoping you would want to redeem yourself, but I should've known you didn't have the guts by the way you acted at my penthouse. I was told you Southern boys lack courage, but I was hoping you'd prove the rumors to be untrue. All you Southerners are the same. Have a nice flight back to Atlanta." Betty slammed the phone before I could respond.

Marcus

I kept telling myself, 'You can't leave this type of negative affect on your first and only visit to LA. I had to make this right before I headed back to Atlanta. I called Betty back and asked," Is there any way I could make this right? "Well, if you're man enough to meet with me before your flight leaves, that might paint a better image for me to consider," said Betty. "Where would you like to meet," I asked. "There's a Coffee Shop at the corner of 'Shanera and Dior Boulevard called 'Kia's Café. Would you like to meet me there in an hour?" Betty asked. Of course. An hour would be perfect, I replied. I called Virgil and asked if he could pick me up an hour earlier than we initially planned. "Sure, I'll be right over," said Virgil.

Marcus

I figured out a way to handle this meeting. I also came up with a plan where Virgil wouldn't be in my business. I plan for him to drop me off approximately two blocks from where I plan to meet Betty. I would then walk the rest of the way. I will inform Virgil that I'd forgotten to purchase a gift for my mom before going back to Atlanta. That way, he wouldn't have any idea of the real reason why I had to come downtown. Looking at things in retrospect, this chauffeur, Virgil, is one of a kind. I've never met anyone who never sleeps. But he's never let me down, so I reckon I should be thankful. On the contrary, Betty was somewhat of a different character. She was as dangerous as she was beautiful. And, in some way, she's connected to my best friend, Edward. I'm not sure if I would be able to talk with Edward face to face before I head back to Atlanta, so I plan to record my meeting with Betty so I could at least show him how dangerous she is, if he doesn't already know. I've got my cellphone set to start recording Betty the minute she and I meet. It's been twenty minutes already, and Virgil, for the first time, is running late. The guy is usually punctual, so I shouldn't hold it against him for being late just once. I am starting to get an eerie feeling about meeting with Betty though. But my ego would not allow me to go back to Atlanta with this woman, thinking I'm some sort of a coward. I finally hear Virgil's limo pulling into Edward's driveway. "Sorry, I'm late, Marcus. I had to make a stop." Not a problem, big guy," I replied. "So, what's up, Marcus?" Well, I totally forgot to grab a gift for my mom, and I know she would be upset if I came back to Atlanta without one," I said. Virgil looked a hot mess. His hair was wild, he was unshaven, and I noticed he seemed rather nervous. I thought perhaps I may have worn the guy out by having him run me back and forth for the better part of four hours. But there was something odd about Virgil; even his hands were shaking noticeably. As we were riding on the interstate, I asked him if I could buy him breakfast. He said, " Thanks, but I don't eat breakfast," brother. I thought to myself, maybe that's the problem. We finally get downtown, and I told Virgil to let me out at the corner, two streets over from where Betty and I agreed to meet. "Virgil, if you don't mind, can you wait in the car, as opposed to going back home and driving back? "Sure, I will be right here until you return, Marcus." I got out of the car and walked two blocks, as I'd planned. I started to have second thoughts about meeting with Betty, but my ego wouldn't let me change my mind.

Marcus

'Meeting With Betty'

I caught a glimpse of Betty's car driving by at low speed. I made sure my phone was set to record our conversation just in case things didn't go right. I remember Betty, much like everyone in LA, isn't one to waste time. As soon as she drove up, the look on her face told me she was dead serious about fulfilling this plan she'd put together. I was merely curious to see how sincere this woman was, and more importantly, I didn't want anyone to think I was some sort of coward. Betty gets out of her car, hands over a large, yellow envelope, and says, "Good morning, Mike, this envelope is for you." I took the envelope from Betty, looked inside, and checked the contents inside the bag. Inside, there were 250,000.00 in 100 Dollar Bills. As a former drug dealer, I knew how to check for authenticity. I checked each bill to make sure the money was real. Sure enough, they were real. I handed the envelope back over to Betty and said to her, "Thanks, but you've got to find someone else to do your dirty work; I'm not interested." Without hesitation, Betty took the envelope, hopped in her car, and drove away. The awkward thing about that whole deal was that Betty didn't even seem upset that I couldn't go through with her business proposition. It seemed I was only a backup to an original plan.

Marcus

'30 Minutes later'

I walked back to where I'd left Virgil supposedly waiting for me in his Limo. But I didn't see Virgil's Limo anywhere. I remember Virgil telling me he would sit in the car until I was done shopping for my mom, but he was nowhere to be found. I called, no answer. I figured he must've gone home for a short minute and fallen asleep. So, I walked back down to Kia's café and purchased a cup of Coffee and a bagel. I tried calling Virgil after I'd done with breakfast but was still unable to reach him. Finally, fifteen minutes later, Virgil pulls up. This was definitely not normal. I've only got an hour and a half before my flight takes off. "Man, what happened? I thought you were going to wait for me in the car, Virgil?" Virgil's hands were shaking out of control. His eyes were as red as the color itself. I started to feel guilty. I thought perhaps my asking him to run me back and forth may have caught up with him. "Are you okay? I asked. I'll be okay. I just need to rest a little," replied Virgil. Why don't you take a rest at Edward's place instead of going across town and coming back to get me, Virgil?" That'll work," said Virgil. We pull up to Edward's driveway. There was something noticeably odd about Virgil. He was in tears. I asked if there was anything I could do to help. "No, brother. I will be fine." I imagined he just needed some rest. We walked inside, and I told Virgil he could crash on the couch. I went in the room so I could get a 15-minute 'power' nap. I was done trying to figure out what was ailing this guy. I checked my phone to see if my meeting with Betty was recorded as I'd planned and to set my alarm to wake me up. I thought it would be a good idea to write a 'Thank You' note for Edward to show my appreciation for everything. While writing, a feeling of discomfort came over me. I wasn't sure what brought about this feeling, but my intuition was telling me something bad was about to happen or had already happened. I peeked out into the living area where Virgil was and realized he'd fallen fast asleep. I wish I could've talked to Edward face to face before leaving, but obviously, he is much busier than I'd imagined.

Marcus

I did manage to get a 'Power Nap' in before my alarm sounded. I got up to check on Virgil immediately. He was wide awoke. And, he looked quite normal after he took a nap. I placed the 'Thank You' note I'd written for Edward on his refrigerator so he'd see it the minute he walked in. Edward and I both have always had good appetites. I know him well enough to say with certainty he will head towards the refrigerator as soon as he walks in. Virgil grabbed my belongings and started to load them in his Limo. I was glad to see Virgil back to his normal self. But oddly, he was still teary-eyed. I decided not to ask him about what seemed to be worrying him anymore. So I locked the doors to Edward's mansion. Then, Virgil and I headed for the Airport. As we were riding along, I thanked Virgil for everything he'd done for me while I was there. "No problem at all, brother," said Virgil

Marcus

'Twenty Minutes later'

As we're heading towards the airport, a sign read, "LAX' Next Right." I was excited in one way and sad in another. Sad for the simple fact I didn't get to speak with Edward as much as I'd like. Particularly, about how dangerous it might be dealing with this side chick, Betty. Also, we didn't get a chance to hang out, not even once. The noise from the airplanes going out and coming in told me we were almost at our destination. The sign now reads, "1 Mile From LAX". Virgil's cell phone starts to ring. Virgil answers, "Hello, who's this? When did this happen, Virgil asks the caller. I'm almost at the airport about to drop Marcus off. But we will turn around right now," Who was that, Virgil?" I asked."That was Veronica. She said Edward had been shot." I was furious. "When and where did this happen? Did Veronica mention it?" I asked. "She just said for us to meet her at the hospital off Sunset Boulevard." I couldn't think straight. My mind was going a thousand miles per hour. Can this car go any faster, Virgil?, I asked. "We're going ninety miles per hour now, brother." Virgil, your speedometer is registered for one hundred twenty, lets make this car do what it says it can, please." Along this drive, I started thinking about the conversation Edward and I had about his co-workers. I thought maybe Edward was caught up in something so big that he couldn't tell me about it. I also started to think that the hour or so Virgil got lost downtown might be something I should wonder about. Or, could it have been someone jealous of how successful Edward was.

I've got all of these questions but don't have a clue where to start.

Marcus

'On The Way to the hospital'

Virgil, did Veronica say if Edward was going to be okay? "She said they wouldn't let her in the hospital because of covid-19." I immediately crossed my fingers and said a silent prayer. After I'd prayed, I asked Virgil What he thought might've happened. "I can't really say. All Veronica said was he was shot with a .38 revolver," said Virgil. I remembered the conversations Edward told me about two or three of his co-workers possessing .38 revolvers. I need to talk with Edward. I'm sure he would tell me who was after him. I just need a minute with him. We pulled into the hospital's parking lot. Veronica, my sister, was soaked in tears. I got out of the car and held her in my arms. "Hey, 'Sis. It's been years. Is he going to make it? I asked. "I don't have a clue. They won't let anyone see him. His wife, Anna B., is scheduled to arrive back from Dubai around 10.30 am. Maybe she can ask the doctors if we could visit him as well," said Veronica. Then I say we sit and wait til she arrives, I replied. "I'm sorry. Veronica, this is Virgil, Edward's driver. "We've met," said Veronica. "My bad. I should've known. My mind is going so fast right now, I can't even think straight, Veronica." Big bruh, I understand, believe me," said Veronica. I looked over at Virgil, who had been rather quiet this whole time. Or should I say unemotional. I didn't know him well enough to judge him, but for someone who told me how much Edward meant to him, he sure has a laid-back way of showing it. But then, who am I to judge? Well, my plan of heading back to Atlanta was definitely out. As we were sitting on a bench outside of the Hospital, an RN was passing by with her note-pad in tow. I stopped and asked her if there were any hotels nearby. "Sir, there's a hotel right across the street from here. It's actually in walking distance," said the nurse. Thank you so much, I replied. "Veronica, I'm going to get a hotel room and stay there for tonight. I would make further plans depending on Edward's health, I said. "I will bring your belongings over, Marcus," said Virgil. It was only 9.00 am. It would be another hour and a half before Edward's wife gets in from Dubai. So meanwhile, I will get a room and try to figure out what I should do. "Marcus, why don't you and I meet back here at the Hospital at 10.40," suggests Veronica. "Sounds like a plan, Sis."

Marcus

'Got A Hotel Room'

I walked over to the Hotel across the street from the Hospital and got a room. Virgil dropped my bags off and left. I sat on the edge of my bed, trying to figure out what must've happened with Edward. My mind kept taking me back to the conversations Edward and I had about the co-workers who possessed .38 revolvers. I remember Edward telling me so many things about his co-workers, but other than that, we didn't get a chance to talk about much else.

Marcus

Twenty Minutes later

As I'm sitting in my hotel room trying to piece together what might've happened with Edward, I hear a sudden knock at my room door. 'Bam, Bam, Bam! Who is it? I asked. Los Angeles Police Department was the response. "How can I help you?" You can help us by opening the door." I opened the door, and the first thing I realized was there were two officers, one standing about 6'8, the other 6'9. "How may I help you, officers?' I asked. The smaller of the two said, "There was a shooting last night. It seems you were at the victim's house when it happened. We would need to take you downtown for questioning, sir," said the officers. "That won't be a problem. Let me first grab my key to my room," I replied. These two cops were definitely the two largest Police Officers I've ever seen in my life. The second thing that threw me for loop was, that these two officers were driving around in a Volkswagon Beetle. There's just enough room for one suspect and the suspect has got to be short and slim. I guess it's my lucky day. I hopped in the back seat and immediately started thinking about the wild stories of police brutality in LA. So, I put in my mind I've got to be as polite as possible. We got to the precinct, and I could hardly stand up. My legs were cramping so badly. One of the officers passed me a bottled water and said, "Hurry up, we don't have all day." I got myself together, stretched for two minutes, and the cramps luckily went away. As I walked up to the precinct, I noticed this candy-apple, Red, souped-up sports car parked in the front entrance. I peeked inside the car as we were walking by and noticed a handgun on the passenger's seat. "You guys must get paid pretty good around here," I said. One officer replied, " That is the Captain's fancy ride. We don't get paid like that," he added. "Quite impressive," I said.

Marcus

The Officers open the door to show me in. The Captain was having a conversation with another officer. "I will be right with you, sir," said the Captain. My mind was still traveling at a thousand miles per hour. The Captain points his finger at me and yells," Sir, I need you to step right up. How can I assist you," he asked. I told the Captain who I was. He immediately says to me, "Don't you say another word. I happen to be Captain Eric Pasco, and I am the head of the LA Police Department. I would like to know where you were last night from 8.00 PM to Midnight. I told the Captain I went out to have a good time, and I got back well after midnight. The Captain asked, "Would you happen to own a handgun, and if so, what type?" I told the Captain I'd never owned a handgun in my life. The Captain questioned me for another two long hours. All of his questions seemed repetitive as if he wanted to try and catch me in a lie. Finally, after two hours of redundant questioning, the Captain said to his officers, "Get him out of my office, boys. Oh, one last thing, Mr. Anderson," I stopped in my tracks. What now? I asked. "You're not off the hook by any means. We will keep an eye on you every move you make. Just keep that in mind," said the Captain. I was more than happy to get away from this Captain. I felt if I'd been questioned any longer, they would've locked me up for strangulation. On the way back to my Hotel, one of the officers asked, "The Captain seemed pretty hard on you back there, ha?" I wanted to tell the officer his Captain is an asshole, but I didn't say anything. I remembered where I was.

Marcus

While we were riding back from the precinct, my mind kept taking me back to my conversation with Edward about his co-workers. As the officers pulled up to my hotel room, they kept reminding me they would be keeping an eye on me throughout my time in LA. I didn't care much about what they were talking about. Hell, I wanted to catch the culprit(s) myself. I checked my watch and realized I was supposed to meet with Veronica at the hospital an hour ago. As soon as the officers let me out, I immediately walked across the parking lot to the hospital, where Veronica was sitting in the lobby with her hands covering her face. "Sis, any news yet? "Marcus, you were supposed to meet me here over an hour ago; how did you forget?" LAPD had me downtown for questioning," I said. "What did you do, brother," asked Veronica. I didn't do anything. Perhaps my staying at Edward's place have them believing I am a suspect as well, I said. "Marcus, Edward passed away an hour ago. And, his wife, Anna B. has been here already. Virgil picked her up from the airport and filled her in on everything that went on. Anna B. has even made funeral arrangements already. Edward's homegoing will be this Sunday at *"Church of Christ"* at 10.00 AM, in Glover Heights. It is Anna B's church. You and I can ride together at the Home-Going. I will pick you up around 9:30 so we can get there early." Sounds like a plan, I said.

Marcus

'Sunday Morning'

Veronica picked me up at 9:30, just as she'd promised. We went over to Anna' B.'s church. It wasn't as packed as I'd anticipated. Never in a million years did I ever think I would be attending a funeral for Edward. I thought he lived his life righteously. Because of the lifestyle I'd chosen, I thought he would be attending a funeral for me. One of the ushers passed me an obituary to view over, but my eyes were so teary I couldn't read it if I had to. I set it down at the pew where I sat. I looked at the entire crowd in attendance. I knew no one other than Veronica. A few minutes later, Virgil arrived. Virgil told me early on he was from Alabama, and on this particular day, his accent was clearly detected. He walked over and asked, "Can I sit with y'all for the time being?" Sure, why not, I replied. The ushers, choir, and pastor slowly walked to the altar. They had arranged for an R&B artist, *'Alexis Johnson'* to perform Edward's favorite gospel song, *"I Won't Complain."* The young woman was extremely talented and gorgeous, I might add.. She sang the song better than the original version. I'm sure Edward was in Heaven smiling after she was done. After the artist finished her song, there were a few people who got up and shared past memories they had with Edward. but I'd never heard of any of them, but my gut feeling told me I should pay attention to everyone, including Virgil. It came time for an unusual, five-minute rendition of The Mighty Clouds of Joy's, *"If Jesus Can't Fix it"* by rising stars, *"Tiny and Tabitha"*, beautiful twin sisters from South Carolina. Every lyric in the song gave me chills. They were equally as talented and beautiful as the first performer, *Alexis*. I wondered what Edward would think if he were in my shoes. There was a part in the song that said, '*That little Boy from California*' really got to me. Even though Edward was from Atlanta, something about that part had me on the edge of my pew. I was so emotional. I couldn't believe Edward was gone forever. He was my only brother. A part of me was devastated, but the other part wanted revenge. I looked over at Virgil, who showed no emotion whatsoever. I thought to myself, this is either one tough guy, or he's connected to my friend's death in some way. I wish I had the skill to read what's on a person's mind, at least for a day.

Marcus

Edward's 'Celebration of Life'

Edward's Home-Going was coming to an end. Even though I was heartbroken, I would have to say the musical performances were the best I've heard. I pray I will be around when all of the performers reach their full potential. I would pay whatever the cost to see these three perform anywhere in the world. As I'm reflecting over me and Edward's friendship, I realize I'd never seen Edward's wife before. I missed their wedding, and Edward didn't have any photos of them together anywhere at his place. "Veronica, while service is coming to an end, I'm going to go over and meet Anna B. and let her know who I am, and if she ever needs anything at all, don't hesitate to give me a call," I said. I think that would be a wonderful idea, Marcus," replied Veronica. I slowly walked over to the front row, where Anna B.' and her relatives were. I didn't know which was Anna B. One of the ushers could tell I needed his assistance. He pointed me in the direction of the woman dressed in Black, with her head down, and the only one whose head was covered by a Black veil. I walked over, knelt down to extend my hand, and introduced myself. I whispered, "I'm sorry for your loss, Anna B. I am Marcus, Edward's best friend from Atlanta, Georgia. I just need you to know that your loss is mine as well. Also, if for any reason you need anything at all, don't hesitate to call me." Anna B. slowly raised her head, lifted her veil, and said, "I know who you are." I couldn't believe my eyes. I was in total shock. I was so confused. I had a few questions for Anna B., but the smirk on her face answered all of them at that very moment. I got up from my knees and slowly walked back to the pew where Virgil and Veronica was sitting. "You look like you just seen a ghost, Marcus," Vernonica said. I wasn't sure how to respond to Veronica's statement. So I kept quiet. As people were lining up to exit. Virgil decided he would go over and talk with Anna B. before service ends. I took this time to share an idea with Veronica.

Marcus

I kept telling myself, 'You've got to get to the bottom of this. I was now certain Anna B. had something to do with Edward's death. I also knew she had to have an accomplice. I figure if she was willing to pay me a quarter of a million dollars to kill him, she wouldn't have done something like this on her own. "Marcus, I can tell your mind is going a hundred miles an hour. Is everything okay, brother?" asked Veronica. Sis, I've got something here I need you to hold for me. "What is it? asked Veronica. "Well, this is a recording. Put it in your purse. If anything happens to me, I want you to listen to it, then turn it over to the Police. I also may have an idea who was involved in Edward's death, I said. "Marcus, you need to be careful. I cannot afford to lose two of my best friends at the same time," said Veronica. No, you won't. You know me better than anyone. So I need you to trust me on this. I've got a plan. I also plan to ride back with Virgil when the service is over. I would like to have a conversation with him," I whispered. "Okay, but again, I need you to be careful," said Veronica. I got this, Sis," I whispered. "Just keep me posted, brother, said Veronica. I will give you a call later on today to let you know what I come up with," I said.

Everyone was exiting the church. I was paying attention to everyone who had an extended conversation with Anna B., which I figured out is actually Betty. Had I read the obituary sooner, I would've seen the 'B' in her name stands for 'Betty. Apparently, when she's away from Edward, she uses her middle name. I notice Virgil and Anna B's conversation is a normal one. Nothing peculiar at all. But I still wanted to question him of his whereabouts on the night my friend was killed. And, ask him if he knows any of the co-workers addresses. Maybe Virgil isn't a suspect at all. I might've foolishly suspected him from the outset because of his past drug addictions. I know Anna'B.'s motive was greed. Even though Edward gave her anything she wanted, it still wasn't enough. But that is just how people are in this world. They're never satisfied. Well, I won't be satisfied either until I find everyone involved in my best friend's death.

Marcus

As Veronica was leaving the church, she and I hugged, and I promised her I would call her before the day was over. Virgil was finally done talking with Anna B. "Are you ready to ride, Marcus?" asks Virgil. Yeah, I'm ready, I replied. "Is there a place where you and I could talk privately, Virgil? " Of course. We can take a ride over to my place. It's peaceful there. I've only got a one-bedroom apartment, but it's clean," Virgil said. As we're riding along, I asked, "Virgil, what will you do now that Edward is gone? " Oh, I got something else lined up," Virgil replied. We arrived at Virgil's one-bedroom apartment. And much to my surprise, it was very clean. He asked if I wanted anything to drink. "No, I'm good, brother. But I would like to use your restroom if it's okay. "Sure, it's down the hallway to the left," said Virgil. My mother always told me, 'You can tell a lot about a person by how they keep their bathroom'. I was hoping Virgil got careless and left some type of evidence that would link him to Edward's death. But this guy's apartment was cleaner than the Board of Health. So, my next plan was to focus on the other co-workers Edward had spoken to me about. I just needed their addresses, which I'm sure Virgil knew where everyone lived. I did notice a rear door next to Virgil's bathroom. I wanted to check it out to see where it goes, but I would have to come up with a hell of an explanation as to why I would be looking around if he were to catch me snooping. So, I ran the water in the bathroom as if I'd used the restroom. Even Virgil's towels were neatly folded and clean. I couldn't find anything that would link Anna B. and Virgil as partners except for the fact that he has been her Chauffeur for many years. I sat back down in Virgil's den room. I asked him if he knew any of Edward's co-worker's addresses. Right when he was about to answer me, Virgil's home phone rang. I haven't seen anyone with a landline in ages. Virgil's phone was on a wall in his kitchen, and apparently, he had left his answering machine on when he went to Edward's homegoing. The phone rang a second time, and before Virgil could pick it up, the caller said, "Virgil, are you there? I was certain it was Anna B. I could recognize her voice anywhere. Virgil picked up the phone, and their conversation lasted about five minutes.

"Still at Virgil's

Marcus

"I hope I didn't intrude on your privacy, brother," I said. "No brother, that was simply a childhood friend from back in the day," replied Virgil. I recall Virgil telling me he doesn't keep up with any of his old friends or family relatives. And, I could recognize Anna B's voice anywhere. So, the fact that he lied about something as simple as that told me he was hiding something.

All of a sudden, a UPS truck drives up. Virgil seemed surprised. "These folks must have the wrong address. I don't order anything online," said Virgil. I immediately sensed something was about to happen. The UPS driver knocks on the door; Virgil opens the door and asks, "What are you here for?" I am delivering something for Virgil Bates, is that you?" asks the driver. "Yes, of course. But may I ask you where it is sent from and who sent it?" Man, look here, I deliver goods. It is not my place to know who sends what. I've got twenty-two other deliveries to make, so you need to sign for this shit so I can keep it moving," said the driver. Virgil, not wanting to piss the driver off any more than he had already, grabs a pen to sign for the delivery. He drops the pen and grabs the seemingly heavy box with both hands. As soon as the driver handed Virgil the item, I immediately told Virgil I had to use his restroom again. I headed for the restroom. All I remember after that was a loud explosion. I was thrown some two hundred yards away and knocked unconscious. When I came to my senses, all I could see was red lights and sirens all over the place, multiple fire trucks, a lot of smoke, an ambulance with 3 or 4 EMTs, and a hearse. As my senses got clearer, I realized the explosion threw me behind a trash dumpster. I felt my legs and arms to see if they were still attached; to my surprise, they were. I am almost certain the UPS driver delivered a bomb that was meant for Virgil. Or, perhaps Virgil and me both. I recall Anna B. calling Virgil minutes before that UPS delivery. I'm almost 100% certain Anna B. had something to do with this. I've got to hitch a ride back to my hotel room.

Marcus

'After the Explosion'

As soon as I got back to my room, I turned on the television, where "Breaking News" was announcing that two occupants at Virgil's address were burnt to a crisp. It was said that the two deceased were so badly burned that they would have to be identified using forensics. And, it is possible; their Identifications still might be inconclusive due to the severity of their bodies. Also, because of the department's heavy backlog, this entire process could take up to a year. So, with that, I was certain Anna B. more than likely believed I was dead, which should work out in my favor. This also means when she sees me again, she will be in for the surprise of her life.

I waited until it was dark. I got dressed in my Black Adidas warm-up suit, which also had Hoody. I wanted to be extra careful. I hitched a ride with a passerby over to Edward's mansion with hopes I would catch Anna B. by surprise, but she wasn't there. I then went with 'Plan B, that if she wasn't there, she would be at her penthouse, which I still don't believe Edward ever knew she had. I went to Edward's garage to retrieve the Red Corvette he told me I could use. As soon as I hit the ignition, it cranked up as if it was waiting for me. I drove over to Anna'B's penthouse. I remember the gate had opening issues, but I also remembered the remedy. I parked the car off the roadway into the bushes. I made sure to wear dark clothing so I wouldn't be easily noticed. I walked up to the driveway. When I got closer, I spotted the Captain's Red, High-performance Sports car I'd seen at the precinct. My first thought was that the captain must be a fast and smart thinker. I assumed he figured out that Anna B. may have had something to do with the bombing at Virgil's. But I wanted to be certain. My intuition told me I should sneak around to that open window in Anna B.'s kitchen to listen in. I crept along to the kitchen window of the penthouse, where Anna B. likes to leave ajar. It sounded as if these two were having a celebration. I thought maybe my mind was playing tricks on me from the explosion. So I went closer to the window so I could listen better. Much to my surprise, Anna B. and the Captain were celebrating and boasting about how well their plan worked to perfection. I could not believe what I was hearing.

Marcus

I knew Anna B. had something to do with Edward's death, but the Captain being an accomplice caught me by surprise. My initial thought was to set the house on fire and kill them both simultaneously. But I was afraid these two devils might escape unharmed. So, I decided to destroy them strategically. I remember at the precinct, a handgun was lying on the passenger's seat of the Captain's car. So I snuck back to the captain's car. I checked the passenger's side door handle, but it was locked. I should've known. I prayed the captain got careless and left the driver's door unlocked. Totally surprised, the door was unlocked. And, the .45 handgun was still sitting in the exact spot I last saw it. I opened the door quietly, grabbed the handgun, and went back to the-open window of the kitchen. My adrenaline was racing like a speeding leer jet. But I had to remain calm and avenge my best friend's death methodically. I could hear the Captain and Anna B. celebrating about how well their plan had worked. I wanted to kill them both instantly, but I didn't want to leave any suspicions. I checked the handgun to make sure it was loaded. I overheard Anna B. say to the captain, "Hun, I'm going to take a hot shower, and when I return, I plan to use your handcuffs, attach your hands to my head board, then make you roar like the badass Lion you are." After hearing that, I decided to wait until Anna B. got in the shower. I remember she likes really hot showers. I knew the mist from the shower would fill the room they were in. I then climbed inside her kitchen and hid beside Anna' B's refrigerator. I also detected Anna B. was very comfortable with undressing in front of the Captain. Which told me this wasn't their first time together. My plan was to be patient, but all of a sudden, I heard the heavy footsteps of the Captain coming towards the kitchen. I got really nervous. I put my finger on the trigger. In my mind, if the captain realizes the window is opened further than it should be, I'm going to have to kill him first and resort to another plan. Luckily for him, he just grabbed a bottle of champagne out of the fridge and headed back to Anna'B.s bedroom.

Marcus

I waited until Anna B. had taken her shower. I knew the room would be misty in a matter of minutes. I waited patiently. I heard the shower slow to a drip. I knew it was almost time. The heat from the shower had the entire penthouse blinded. I heard Anna B. say to the Captain, "Sweety, you can have me however you like now. I am as fresh as a ripe tomato," said Anna B.." I like the sound of that," replied the Captain. I started walking boldly toward their voices. I checked again to make sure the Captain's gun was loaded. My plan was to shoot Anna B. first so it would look like a Murder-Suicide. Then shoot the Captain in his right temple and place the .45 in his right hand, as if he'd committed the murder and then turned the gun on himself. But more importantly, I first wanted them both to look me in the eyes before I killed them. I opened Anna B's half-closed room door. "I think you two may have underestimated me," I said. Anna B. jumped up like she'd seen a ghost. I shot her right between the eyes. I then looked the Captain in the eyes. "Marcus, brother, we can work this out. Anna B. put me up to this whole thing. We can split the money fifty-fifty. It's all right here under this mattress," said the Captain. Captain, I plan to let you go free, but before I do, I've got a few questions I need to ask you," I said. I could see the sense of easement in the Captain's eyes. "I will answer whatever you need me to; just don't kill me," said the Captain. I unlocked the cuffs from the headboard so he would feel a sense of relief. "First off, Captain, what money are you talking about, and where did it come from?" I asked. " Anna B made a withdrawal from one of her husband's accounts." I need you to show me this money you're speaking of," I said. The Captain stood up, lifted the mattress, and sure enough, there were stacks of Hundred Dollar bills neatly lined in a suitcase under the mattress. "Okay, Captain, I need you to remain standing. "What do you plan to do to me, brother?" asked the Captain. Just relax, Captain. I am trying to make this whole thing make sense. "Do you own any other handguns, Captain?" No, I do not. However, I do own a .45 similar to the one you have pointed directly at my head, though," said the Captain. So, which one of you killed Edward, Captain? "Edward Keats was shot and killed by Gino Sanchez, a member of a gang out of Oakland called" The Heart-Stoppers," a supposedly non-violent gang consisting of mostly teens from poverty-stricken neighborhoods. However, I personally had Gino under surveillance the moment he moved here in LA. He was wanted for another murder he committed in San Fransisco but had slipped out of sight from law enforcement. So, when I heard he'd just moved here, I personally had him under my radar. I didn't tell any of my officers because I didn't want anyone to blow my cover. Anna B. happened to run into Gino at the same grocery store twice in the same week. The second time they met, they struck up a long conversation. When it comes to money, Anna B. would do whatever it took to have it. She wanted her husband dead, so it didn't matter who it was that would be willing to do the task. Without ever researching Gino, she offered him ten thousand dollars to kill her husband. Of course, he took her up on the offer, but little did Anna B. know he would've killed for nothing. Gino was a straight-up 'Killer," said the Captain.

Marcus

'The Confession'

"If Anna B. had done her research, she could've saved money," said the Captain. So, where can I find this Gino now? I asked. "You won't find him anywhere," said the Captain. When Gino and Anna B. made the money transaction, I video recorded it and was planning to Blackmail Anna B., but I remembered Gino rode his bike over to meet with Anna B. that night. I watched him put the money in his backpack and rode off. I called one of my officers and lied to him that I'd just witnessed a Hispanic guy stealing out of a grocery store on 38th Street. I gave him a description of Gino and told my officer the suspect was on a bike. I had the officer stop Gino as soon as he got to the dark portion of his route home. The officer held Gino there until I got there. I then told my officer I wanted him to investigate another incident in progress at the corner of 49th and Sunset Boulevard. When my officer left, I searched Gino's bag, took the money, killed him, and threw him in the Ocean. Afterward, I came over here to Anna B's penthouse to present the recorded video of their scheme, but when I mentioned to her I had incriminating evidence against her, she offered me half of what she had under her mattress. I wasn't sure how much it was, but when I saw it, I was certain it was a lot more than I'd plan to Blackmail her for," said the Captain. Okay, but why the explosion at Virgil's place? I asked. "Marcus, that bomb was meant for you and Virgil both. Anna B. had paid Virgil 5,000.00 cash upfront to kill you the Saturday morning before you headed back to Atlanta, but Virgil reneged on the deal. He smoked it all up and was too high to follow through on the plan. So, Anna B. and Virgil had agreed that he would repay her incrementally until the balance was taken care of. But earlier today, when she called Virgil so they could set up the payment dates, her mindset changed immediately when Virgil told her he couldn't discuss the matter because you were at his house. Anna B. got so upset that she totally lost it. She immediately arranged to have a bomb sent to kill you both. She wanted you two dead for different reasons. She wanted you dead because she sensed during her husband's funeral you might've had her figured out, and she knew Virgil would've never been able to repay her because of his addiction. So getting rid of both of you at once seemed like a perfect plan, I'm sure," said the Captain. Interesting story you made up, Captain," I said. "Oh no, brother, that is not a made-up story; that was the plan, Marcus," said the Captain. We're almost finished here, Captain. Just a few more questions before I let you go free. "Captain, did you know Edward at all, I asked. "Not at all. I never met him. Not even once," said the Captain. Now, how long were you on the force?" I asked. "Twenty-seven long years," said the Captain. During any of those Twenty-Seven years, did you ever have to share anything with a dead person, Captain? With a puzzled look on his face, the Captain replied, "I don't recall ever having to do such a thing," replied the Captain. "Neither will I, Captain." I shot the Captain on the right side of his temple and placed his .45 in his right hand. His heavy torso hit the wall so hard that it knocked down every framed picture that was hanging in Anna B's bedroom.

Marcus

I then took all the cash they had stored under Anna B's mattress and headed back to the kitchen window to make my exit. I realized the two framed poems, "*Incognito*" and "*Love,*" Anna B. had hanging in the hallway, had fallen down as well. I couldn't recall if I'd ever touched them with my hands during my first visit, so I wanted to make sure I wouldn't leave any loose ends. So, I picked them up, wiped them off thoroughly for fingerprints, and as I was about to hang them back on the wall, I looked at the back and almost broke down in tears. Each had been signed, "Poem by "Ed the Great! I never would've guessed it. I hung the poems back, wiped off everything my hands might've touched throughout the entire house, hopped through Anna B's kitchen window, and walked back to Edward's Vette. I got on the interstate and drove over 2,400 miles back to Atlanta GA.

"Incognito"

'If I were an artist
I would do a painting of her face on Black canvas,
Just so I could meticulously capture the beauty in her silky-
smooth skin tone;
I would use an ultra-thin brush to be certain not even a
millimeter of her lips would go unnoticed.
I would also use enamel paint,
Which would perfectly depict just how bright and gorgeous her
smile is;
I would cleverly paint her eyes in a way that
Her charming personality could be seen through them;
I might even add an amazing sunset to the painting so folks
could see how close in comparison her eyes are to a sunset;
I would then place my painting on top of Mount Everest,
So folks could look through my eyes and have hope,
Hope that they too could be serendipitous
and stumble into someone they might find equally as beautiful
and amazing that they would fall for as well;
And at the very end of my painting
I would leave it signed, "Anonymous"
So, folks would be equally as mystified about the artist
As they would be not knowing who she is.'

"Love..."

I remember you.
I was so very young when I encountered you for the first time.
I was at an age where, had I fallen for you, everything would've seemed foreign, and going out of my way to find out what you were about seemed like a risk my young heart was not prepared to chance.
I was definitely intrigued but too afraid to give in.
My biggest fear may have been whether or not I'd been able to fulfill any high expectations you might've asked of me.
But that was then.
I've since grown astronomically, and those fears I once had no longer exist.
Even though I know your presence would have an impact similar to that of a swirling tornado, I fear nothing.
I've also acquired a better understanding of your purpose.
So if you are as soothing and comforting as I have imagined, I would like for us to meet again.
Not just for the sake of reigniting what was once at the very tip of my fingers but so I could freely open up and allow you access to the key that would safe-lock my heart.

Marcus

'Six Months Later'

I bought an old abandoned building and had it converted into a restaurant. I had it gutted out, then restored, and six months later, I opened my restaurant and Cigar Bar in the heart of Buckhead. However, I would have the official Grand Opening two weeks later. I thought it would be something Edward would be proud of if he was still alive. I named the place 'Three of Us' Cigar Bar and Grill,' an honor to both Edward and our sister, Veronica. I never got an opportunity to touch base with Veronica before I left California. I survived that explosion but lost my cell phone in the process. That day of the explosion at Virgil's, the' LA @ 5News' reported two bodies had been burnt so badly the coroner said their identities would be almost impossible to make out. So, I'm sure Veronica tried calling me several times, but I had no way of contacting her. I'm sure she thinks I, along with Virgil, were the ones that got fried to a crisp that day. I mailed her a thousand dollars and sent her plane tickets along with the invitation. She knows me as well as anyone. I'm almost certain she will be here. Perhaps I will explain everything when she gets here, or maybe not. I'm hoping she would be so overwhelmed about being announced as co-owner of this establishment that she may not even ask about what happened on that particular day.

Marcus

'Two Weeks Later at The Grand Opening'

I had arranged for Edward's mother, LaDonna, Veronica's mom, Sarah, and my mother, mama Johnson, to sit at the head of the table. Next to them, I had arranged for myself and Veronica to be seated side by side. Veronica was late, but she arrived nonetheless. The most important thing of all was she did arrive safely. The entire place was full to capacity. About 200 hundred people showed up from everywhere. My entire former crew from the band came out. Even Steve, my old band manager, came to show some love. When I got on stage to thank everyone for coming out, my emotions got the best of me. I had to take a fifteen-minute pause to get my nerves together. As I looked around in the audience, I almost could hear Edward saying, "I'm proud of you, Marcus. And thank you for that last favor." I got myself together, and for the first time in my life, I had a meaningful announcement to make.

"First and foremost, I'd like to thank everyone for coming out. This 'Opening' was an idea I had for a long time. But it couldn't have happened if it weren't for God and two very special friends in my life. Unfortunately, one of them couldn't be here tonight, but I know he's listening. The origin of the name "Three of Us' Cigar Bar and Grill' was created by me with my two best friends in mind. I am referring to the late Edward Keats and my sister, Veronica DuBose, who knows me better than I know myself. Veronica was invited here tonight, not only because she was always a loyal friend, but she is also the co-owner, along with myself, of this new establishment. (Audience gives a standing ovation)., I would also like to thank the Buckhead community for allowing us the opportunity to serve with Pride, Dignity, and Professionalism. Our hours of operation are Monday through Sunday, from 4.00 pm til midnight. In honor of Mr. Edward Keats, we will have Spoken Word Every Friday and Saturday night from 7.00 p.m. to 10.00 p.m. And lastly, I would like everyone to have a great time, but please don't drink and try to drive home. We've got a Courtesy van that will escort you home if you may have had too much to drink. Thank you all once again for coming out. Now, let's eat, party, and have a good time!

"The End"